FIRE OVER
TROUBLED WATER

DROWNED EARTH

DROWNED EARTH

Eight novellas.
Eight Australian authors.
One watery apocalypse.

Scientists said that it would take 5000 years for Earth's oceans to rise.

They were wrong.

After an asteroid collides with Antarctica, a tsunami devastates the world's coastal cities and escalates the melting of the ice caps.

These eight novellas set in various locations around Australia explore the potential consequences of such a catastrophe. They can be read in any order.

FIRE OVER
TROUBLED WATER

NICK MARONE

DROWNED EARTH

First published by Deadset Press in 2019

www.aussiespeculativefiction.com

ISBN: 978-0-6484211-1-5

Cover design Copyright © Alanah Andrews

Edited by Alanah Andrews & Austin P. Sheehan

www.aussiespeculativefiction.com

DEDICATION

To my parents, for all the encouragement, and to my fellow card night players, because you asked for it.

CHAPTER ONE

One single bolt of lightning pierced the seascape astern of *Mara*, thunder rumbling over the water a few seconds later. Baz looked back at the approaching storm front, realising it was pushing his way faster than he'd previously thought. At best, it would hit his boat within the hour.

The water rocked his boat so much it would make an onlooker seasick. Even the gusty wind grew colder. The wind ahead of the storm drove off the characteristic heat that had plagued the New South Wales South Coast islands after the Rise, and it made sailing a wind-powered vessel that much harder.

It also put Baz's life at risk.

The booming thunder snapped Baz's mind into gear. His charts showed there was no way he would reach Narooma Island before the storm rolled over him. No land was visible to the naked eye, and even if there was land in view, he wouldn't want to risk approaching it without first studying the shoreline. The only option was to weather the storm exactly where *Mara* sat.

His muscles ached as he reefed the sails so as not to catch too much wind. Then he set up his storm jib. It would allow him to keep moving at a slow pace and better negotiate the big waves that were sure to come. He went to the ornate timber wheel and turned *Mara* about to face the storm, bobbing over swells and heaving against the wind, hoping—like he'd hoped countless times before—that he and his sailing trawler would live to see the next day . . . that he would live to continue his search for his daughter and grandchildren.

He remembered to attach his harness to the safety bar next to the wheel just before a wave reached *Mara*'s bow. The solid vessel rose with the wave, paused all forward motion at the crest, and then plunged downward into the trough. The movement mimicked a brief moment of weightlessness, causing Baz's stomach to turn. Foam splashed across the deck as the bow slammed into the water at the bottom. Baz gripped the wheel for dear life, deciding it was definitely the worst storm he'd been in.

The approach to the next wave tipped *Mara* slightly to starboard and Baz fought to regain a level heading before meeting the wave head-on. The resulting thump of the wave against *Mara*'s hull halted the trawler and pushed it backwards. The watery beast rolled on under Baz's boat and mercifully dropped him over the other side, where *Mara* sat idle until the storm jib pushed her along again.

The sea was a lot more forgiving for a moment after that. Baz had enough time to take one hand off the wheel and wipe the sea spray from his face with a wet sleeve, chuckling maniacally at the uselessness of the act. He found it strange that he could laugh at a time like this.

A sheet of rain steadily moved in his direction— as if the situation wasn't already bad enough. Another incoming wave loomed ahead of him, this one off his port bow, forcing him to turn into it. The crest was nearly as high as his mainmast, but he attacked it nevertheless— he had no choice. As he reached the top, the rain swept across his position and drenched the deck so much that when *Mara* tipped downwards towards the trough, a heavy stream of rainwater seeped into the deckhouse. He made the mistake of adjusting his footing at this moment, and the sudden change in pitch made him slip, accidentally turning the wheel as a result. *Mara* tipped down the wave at an angle and then lurched to starboard as she met the trough. The movement nearly made Baz stumble again, but he regained his footing and steadied his beloved vessel.

The rain had cut visibility, but by this point, Baz didn't care. He knew he would have to fight the tempest no matter how little he could see or for however long it lasted. He just hoped that this battle wouldn't be his last.

CHAPTER TWO

Narooma Island was nothing like its namesake—the submerged town not five kilometres to the south. Baz, exhausted and still saturated after weathering the storm, sailed *Mara* to a makeshift wharf. It was crudely constructed out of hewn logs and roughly milled timber planks. He threw a line out to a waiting Islander, who promptly tied his boat to the wharf. The grey planks wobbled under his feet as soon as he stepped off his boat.

"It's fine, trust me," the Islander said. "I walk on it all the time." He extended a hand. "Rick."

"Baz." Despite his fatigue, he made certain to give a firm handshake. "I've come from Flat Rock with water to barter."

Rick's eyes lit up. "Flat Rock, eh? I thought your boat looked a step up from the rest."

Baz's trawler was a heavily modified desalinisation vessel. Pipes ran along each side of the hull, and there were two protruding tanks at the bow and stern. Even his sail design had been adjusted to account for the extra weight and draught changes when carrying a full load.

"So what excess do you have to trade?" Baz asked him.

Rick scratched his chin. "Mate, not much. We're struggling here. But we do have plenty of apples and honey. Hopefully this time next year we'll have more variety."

Baz frowned and thought about the list of things his mayor had asked him to find. Flat Rock was doing well enough for fruit and vegetables. They didn't have apples growing on the island, so maybe he could get some for consumption and planting. But honey . . .

"How do you package the honey?" Baz asked. He wanted to figure out how to measure the value of his water in honey.

"Oh, in whatever we can find—glass or plastic jars, tubs, even bottles. We're actually running out of containers to store honey in, so quite a bit goes to waste."

And there was Baz's opportunity. He put on his best thoughtful face. "I'm willing to sell you water in exchange for honey. But, since you say you produce too much honey, would you also consider selling a hive?"

"Ah, *that* I'm not sure about. But we can ask. Come on, I'll take you up to the apiary." Rick turned to a girl who was sitting on a rock near the wharf. "Hey, Shelly! Watch the wharf, will you."

"Okay, Dad."

"Your boat'll be all right. Come on, the apiary's not far."

Rick began to walk and Baz followed, looking back at his trawler and the little girl who had waltzed over and was dancing barefoot on the wharf. He smiled sadly at her playfulness, but a pain in his heart made him look away.

They passed clusters of buildings made from whatever materials were available—mostly logs and mud. It was the best the Islanders could do, unlike those in the cities, who still had the top sections of skyscrapers for shelter. Then again, survivors such as those on Narooma Island had room to grow their own food. Not much of it, though, Baz saw. The island seemed to be failing at communal farming. Maybe it was bad management, maybe it was a lack of skills. Baz didn't know and he didn't think much of it. Instead, he studied the face of

7

every woman he saw, hoping for the thousandth time that he'd spot his daughter.

When Baz found himself dodging bees in mid-flight, he knew they were getting close to their destination. Homemade beehives sat under and around a copse of trees on a gentle slope of land. Walking among them was a lone woman wearing shorts and the sleeves of her T-shirt rolled up to her shoulders, apparently comfortable with the thousands of bees coming and going around her.

"Deidre!" Rick called, and the middle-aged woman faced them. "This bloke's a merchant. He wants to buy a hive."

Deidre looked at Baz with a contorted face. "Are you for real?"

Baz was taken aback by the woman's aggressive response. "Yeah, I am. Why?"

She took a few steps towards him. "I just never heard of anyone wanting to move an entire hive across the water," she told him, wiping a bead of sweat from her forehead. "You're better off finding a local swarm. Where are you taking them, anyway?"

"Flat Rock."

Deidre raised her eyebrows and tilted her chin up at the mention of the South Coast's most successful island community. "Oh, I see."

8

Baz's mission wasn't just to barter goods for the betterment of his island. If he could foster good trade relationships with the surrounding islands, then when the time came to barter bigger, smarter, more valuable items, the existing trade partners would be more inclined to take advantage of Flat Rock's productivity. At least that was what Flat Rock's mayor, Bev Greenfield, believed.

"I'd be happy to pay your price for a hive, and some extra for you to teach me how to transport it properly and set it up at home."

Deidre scrunched her mouth in thought, while Rick, obviously not the one to negotiate anything, studied the bees zipping in and out of a nearby box.

"What do you have to trade?" Deidre asked.

"I have about two-thousand litres of fresh water on my trawler, with the ability to desalinate more if you wish. Apart from that, I can return to Flat Rock with a list of things your island needs and bring back what I can."

Deidre licked her lips. "Well, I know we need water." She paused and looked away, back towards the main village. "I think you should talk to our Overseer. He's got a better idea of what things are worth and what we need. Rick, would you find Noah?"

Rick nodded and darted off to the village. Now alone together, Baz and Deidre got into a lively discussion about the benefits of bees and honey. She told him how to care for them, where to position hives, and how to transport them. It was clear that bees were her passion, and Baz was happy to see someone who had adjusted so smoothly since the Rise. Too many people complained about their situation and wished for years gone by, but Baz knew there was no point. The water would always be a part of everyone's lives now. The best thing to do was to deal with it—embrace it, even.

"I could come back with you and help you set up the hive . . . if you do buy one," Deidre said. She smiled warmly.

Baz's heart sank, knowing he would have to explain the situation yet again. "Look, I'm sorry, but Flat Rock has a strict immigration policy. There's a good chance you wouldn't be allowed in."

Deidre's shoulders slumped. "Yeah, so I've heard," she said softly.

It broke Baz's heart to see her reaction. He'd seen the same despondent look on countless villagers and islanders throughout the South Coast whenever he shot down their hopes of a better life. He tried to tell himself that he was saving them the trouble of making the trip to Flat Rock, only to be turned back upon arrival.

Soon enough, Rick returned with Narooma's overseer, an elderly man named Noah.

Noah shook Baz's hand with a limp, shaky grip and spoke in a croaky voice. "I hear you have water for us?"

"That's right."

"And you want to buy honey, do you?"

"Yes," Baz said with a nod. "And a beehive, if I may."

Noah chuckled hoarsely and waved at the hives beside them. "We do have plenty to spare, don't we, Deidre?"

"Yep," Deidre replied, but without much enthusiasm.

Still chuckling, Noah looked back at Baz. "We'll take four-thousand litres of water, and we need these items." He handed Baz a short, thin timber plank with items written in pencil. "For those items, we'll be happy to trade our own excess produce. Is Flat Rock in a position to trade continuously?"

Baz put on his best diplomatic face. "I think thirty merchant vessels and counting shows we are in a good position for long-term trade." He regarded the list. "Yes, Mayor Greenfield should be happy with this. I'll give you your water and take back a hive as a show of goodwill—to get the trading started. Then you'll have Flat Rock boats visit you soon to fulfil the rest of this order. After that, you'll be in the system for regular trading runs."

"Sounds like a deal," Noah said. He stepped forward and shook Baz's hand again, more firmly this time.

Just like that, Baz had set up another trade route for Flat Rock Island. But the real reason why he bothered to do it sat constantly on his mind, gnawing away at him.

CHAPTER THREE

Calm weather prevailed while Baz desalinised the next two-thousand litres of water for the people of Narooma Island. All he had to do was sail offshore and suck up water into his now empty tanks, where his system would do its work. *Mara*'s gentle rocking motion nearly put him to sleep.

It was almost dusk when he returned to Narooma with full tanks of fresh water. He took turns with some of the fitter men to manually pump the water out of his tanks and into the village's supply tanks. The whole process took a long time, and by the end of it, Baz's back and muscles were sore. He asked Noah if he could sleep on his trawler while it was berthed at the wharf. Noah, who had become quite amicable and still surged with energy, insisted that Baz sleep in the comforts of one of the village huts, but Baz was sure his cabin on the trawler was more comfortable. And besides, he didn't want to leave *Mara* unattended at night.

The next morning's sunrise was blocked by a dense fog. Baz woke up chilled and fetched a worn jumper his daughter had bought for him many years ago. He paused when he picked it up, studying its holes and tears. He thought about Suzie every time he saw it, which was why he left it on the trawler. It was a tangible reminder of his mission.

Baz wandered through the fog on the island, trying to find the beehives again. "Dammit," he muttered to himself as he turned one way and then the other in the dense fog. Then there was a disturbance in the mist and, as Baz watched, Noah appeared. When asked which way to go, the old man looked in one direction, into the grey-white mist, and pointed, like it was so obvious that the bees were in that direction. He thanked Baz again for the trade arrangements they had made, before moving on.

The sound of footsteps crunching bark hit Baz's ears when he reached the first beehive, but he couldn't see who it was.

A voice called out, "Who's there?"

"Hey, Deidre—it's me, Baz. Where are you?"

"At the hut in the middle of the hives."

Baz weaved his way between the hives, wafting through the fog, which seemed to have grown thicker. Deidre was on her knees searching through drawers in the hut when he arrived. She mumbled a greeting but didn't look up. Then she stood, holding some netting and a heavy staple gun. "Let's prepare a hive for transport."

They stepped outside and got to work. Being early morning and quite cool, the bees were still in their hives. Baz was supposed to transport them overnight, but his fatigue necessitated him staying put, which meant he'd have to move them through the day. He assured Deidre that he had a cool spot on his boat, for she was concerned about their survival. They continued their discussion on beekeeping while they worked, but the topic changed soon after they began.

"So," Deidre started, "have you always been a part of Flat Rock?"

Baz could see where the conversation might lead, but he went along with it. "No, I'm originally from Ulladulla. I went to Flat Rock just as the settlement was established."

"Oh. And they let you in?"

Baz's lips curled into a smile and he sniffed a laugh. "Yeah, but back then things weren't so tight. We had no mayor, no immigration rules, and nobody to *enforce* rules, even if we did have them."

Deidre started covering the entrance to the hive with the netting. "Then why is it so different now?"

"Well, it's like this. Mayor Greenfield is in charge now, and what she says, goes. She's a bit paranoid about managing the island's resources and keeping disease out. Those are probably the two main reasons why it would be hard for you to get in. It's because you're an outsider. Back when I moved in, it was a free-for-all. Now the situation is more controlled."

After tying the netting to the hive's entrance, Deidre downed her tools and rested on the dewy grass. "So that means absolutely nobody can get in anymore? That's a bit cruel if you ask me."

Yeah, I know, Baz thought sadly. "We turn a lot of people away," he said aloud, "but that doesn't stop them from coming. I'm sorry if I was short with you about it yesterday."

"No, that's okay. I guess you were just doing your job."

"Yeah," Baz answered, and the conversation lulled into an awkward silence. The work on the hive was done, but Deidre wasn't moving. Baz decided to explain the situation a bit more. "It's actually harder for someone to leave Flat Rock than it is for someone to gain entry, if that makes you feel any better."

Deidre shot him a quizzical look.

"You see, once you're a citizen of Flat Rock, the rules say you can never emigrate away from the island. It's just the way it is. We have skills that we need—skills that help us grow and develop and build stuff for export. Mayor Greenfield doesn't want any of those skills leaving the island. But she does sometimes accept skilled workers into Flat Rock. It's rare, though."

At that, Deidre's eyes went wide. "But I have skills. I'm an apiarist. Look at what I've done here." She held her arms out, gesturing at all the beehives within view in the fog.

Baz sighed. He liked Deidre. She was a nice lady and he could see that she really wanted to leave Narooma for someplace better. He couldn't tell what her loss would mean for Narooma, but maybe it wouldn't be so bad. She had already set up an apiary, and maybe she had trained or was training someone else to share the load. Baz wanted to help her.

"I'll tell you what I'll do," Baz began. "Let me go home and speak to Mayor Greenfield. We don't have an apiarist, and I'm sure she would be interested in setting up something like this on the island." He, too, pointed at all the hives around them. "If she says yes, I'll organise for a trader to come and get you. How does that sound?"

Her mouth dropped open. "You would do that for me?"

Baz nodded. It felt good to make the promise. His mind was already racing with the arguments he would put to Mayor Greenfield.

"Thank you," she said. Then she laughed. "Thank you."

"It's all right," Baz told her with his hand up. "I see too many people pushed away from Flat Rock. It's good to do something about it, for a change. But I need to keep moving, so we should take this hive to the wharf if it's ready."

They carried the hive to *Mara*, where Baz loaded it in a safe spot. Noah was there with Rick and some other villagers who had played a role in the trade. Baz shook hands with all of them, promising a merchant would return in a few days to complete their transactions. But before he left, he asked for a private word with Noah. The old man pulled Baz aside and bent close to listen to what he had to say.

Baz looked over both shoulders before speaking. "Do you have a woman here by the name of Susan, or Suzie, Cosgrove? She'd be in her mid-thirties."

Noah stroked his grey beard. "We do have a Susan on the island, but she's living with a man named Bill Humphries. So she calls herself Suzie Humphreys. I don't know what her real surname is."

The name "Bill Humphreys" didn't mean anything to Baz. Suzie's husband, Troy, had died in floodwaters shortly after the Rise. That was when Baz lost contact with her. Whatever the situation, Baz had to check it out for himself. "I need to see her before I go. You see, I'm looking for my daughter. Does this Susan have children?"

"Oh, yes, several," Noah said with his characteristic chuckle. He motioned for Baz to come with him. They walked up to the village. "The eldest kids are very helpful around here, but the younger ones are brats. Frankly, I think they need some discipline—a good smack when they do wrong to teach them that wrong is wrong. I think . . ."

Baz wasn't listening. All he wanted to do was see the woman for himself.

By this time in the morning, the sun was burning through the fog. A bright blue day poked through the wisps of moisture. Noah approached a strongly-built man who was chopping a tree down with an axe and called out to him.

"Bill! How are you, mate?"

19

"Good, Noah," Bill replied. He left the axe buried in the tree trunk and turned to face the two approaching men.

"Is Susan about?" Noah asked.

"Yeah, she should be at home in the veggie patch."

"All right, thanks. Take care, mate."

Noah led Baz away under the watchful eyes of Bill. It wasn't until they were some distance away that Baz heard the axe attacking the tree again. Down a dirt path, between rows of shabbily built huts, Noah pointed to where Bill and Susan lived and called Susan's name as he approached.

"Is that you, Noah?" It was a soft voice coming from behind the hut. Baz hadn't heard his daughter's voice for so many years—he was ashamed to admit that he'd forgotten what she sounded like.

A woman appeared at the side of the shack and greeted Noah and Baz, and that was when Baz's heart sank. Standing before them was a woman with Asian features whom Baz suspected was an Australian with Chinese heritage. There had been a lot of Chinese families moving to Sydney and Canberra in the years before the Rise, and it was reasonable to assume that some moved to the South Coast or were at least caught there after Jagannatha struck. But it was abundantly clear that this Susan wasn't Baz's daughter.

"I'm sorry, Miss," Baz said. "I'll let you get on with your day." He retreated up the road, leaving Noah to catch up.

"Not her, eh?"

"No."

"Sorry, mate. But it was worth a try, wasn't it?"

"Yeah." Baz stopped walking, turned his face to the sun and felt its warmth. "Look, I'll be leaving now. You don't have to accompany me to the wharf. Maybe I'll be back here someday and we can have a drink." He shook Noah's hand again.

"I like the sound of that. And thank you for everything, Baz."

They parted, Baz retracing his steps to the wharf. He pulled off his jumper before he got there, for the morning was already warming up. Then he untied *Mara*, unfurled his sails, and pulled away from Narooma, wondering, hoping, praying that his daughter was still out there somewhere.

CHAPTER FOUR

It was a day and a half's sail from Narooma to Flat Rock, smooth enough, with a strong breeze to push Baz along. Off in the distance, there was a thin band of dark cloud between the blue-white sky and blue-green sea, though there was no sound of thunder. All things considered, what with the Rise and all, Baz found beauty in the waters he traversed. There was something serene about being alone on the water, carried by the wind, rising and falling with the movement of a gentle sea. Baz was of the age and experience that he didn't care for anyone's crap anymore, and he had few people to deal with when he was out sailing. That was just the way he liked it.

He passed a few boats on his voyage home. Some were Flat Rock traders, and they exchanged waves and taunts of friendly competition. Others were refugee boats. Baz saw too many refugee boats in his time on the water. But now and then a different boat would come into view. One such boat sailed directly towards Baz, and he stiffened when he realised what it was.

"Hey there," one of the men on the boat called as they slowed beside him. "Do you know the way to Batemans Bay?"

Baz put on his best fake smile and pointed in the right direction. "There's a large buoy a few hours that way. The town is directly underneath it." Yes, just as he suspected, these men were looters. One of them sat at the stern of their pristine vessel, servicing some diving gear.

"Thanks, buddy," the looter said, grinning. Then he cast his eyes over Baz's strange boat. "Say, where are you from?"

It was a question asked often enough that Baz had an answer prepared for it. "I'm just a surveyor out from Sydney," he said, hoping his short reply would end the conversation.

"Righteo. Well, safe travels. Maybe we'll see you when we get back."

Don't count on it. "Sure, you never know. Best of luck with your diving—I hope you find something."

The guy laughed. "We will. We always do."

With that, the two parties went their separate ways, Baz happy to see the back of them. He didn't want anyone following him home unless they were Sydney traders with something worth selling.

Later that day, the island which had become his home appeared as a thin dark line on the horizon. In a few hours, Baz was sailing past Flat Rock's sparsely-inhabited east coast. In the past, the area was known as Flat Rock State Forest, but since the Rise, the new residents called it Flat Rock Island, or simply Flat Rock. Much of the blackbutt eucalypt forest was still in its pre-flood state. The Islanders generally used the hardwood for building, though Baz knew of one couple who were trying to build an old-fashioned paper mill and learn the craft—blackbutt was supposedly a good raw material for paper production.

A sailing ketch patrolled the east coast of the island. Guardsmen studied Baz's boat as he sailed past, then returned to their duties on the ketch when they recognised him. Greenfield maintained a twenty-four-hour watch on the island's perimeter and had given the Flat Rock Guard all the vessels they needed to fulfil that important commission.

As Baz rounded the island to sail along the north coast, he saw a long, rundown vessel being escorted out to sea by one of Flat Rock's radio-controlled drones. He quickly checked that his Flat Rock ensign was flying so he could be easily identified and not fired on by the sometimes trigger-happy drone pilots. The passengers on the refugee boat looked downcast and scared, but none of those feelings had ever swayed Mayor Greenfield. A minute number of people had been allowed to immigrate to the island. That small number gave everyone else a shred of hope.

The fact was, Greenfield technically owned the land on which Flat Rock Island's town had started. She was a widow when the Rise occurred, and she kindly offered her land to the fleeing residents of the lower-lying areas closer to the coast. Her land consisted of a cleared area adjoining the north-eastern side of Flat Rock State Forest. Since she was the landowner of that large, arable, and buildable patch, the new residents voted her mayor, and she had held that title ever since.

Big mistake, Baz thought with a frown. Even though Flat Rock had done quite well for itself—becoming the envy of the South Coast—it was a law unto itself. With the general breakdown of civilisation in the South Coast, the survivors had to make sense of their new reality and move on. No longer was the New South

Wales government able to run things from their offices in Sydney, nor did the Federal decisions from Canberra matter to anyone anymore. It seemed the whole country as a unit was falling apart and replaced with splintered groups forming governments and societies of their own. Flat Rock was one of them, and Greenfield decided to help others only inasmuch as helping others would help herself and Flat Rock.

The refugee boat was well on its way out to sea and the drone now flew over Baz's trawler. It hovered there, its little camera focusing on the tanned man at the wheel, dual pistols mounted either side of the camera. Baz gave the drone a middle finger and grinned devilishly before it turned and zipped back towards the island's dock.

There was a bay on the northern side of the island which acted as the sole entry and exit point for Flat Rock. Baz sailed into it, looking up at one of the observation towers to port. This was where the drone operators did their work, and he was pleased to see that the operator for the north zone was none other than Ivan Zimmer, the man who built the island's radio tower, modified the drones for solar power, figured out how to attach and fire the drones' pistols, and trained the other operators. Greenfield granted him citizenship on the island when he came to her with his brilliant island reconnaissance and defence idea. The balding Zimmer flipped his middle finger at Baz with a laugh, returning the gesture. That made Baz chuckle. He liked Zimmer—the man had a wicked sense of humour.

When Baz berthed at one of the piers reserved for local trading vessels, he saw that Mayor Greenfield was waiting for him, arms folded, looking cross.

"What have I done?" Baz asked her as he threw a rope to a dockworker.

"Where's all your produce? Huh? Gone for days and you bring nothing back?" She stomped right up to the trawler as it nudged the side of the dock, her grey hair swaying with her movements.

Baz simply stood behind the wheel and shrugged. "Hey, I negotiated a good deal. He stamped his foot and pointed at the deck, grinning. "And Narooma is now part of our trading route." He could see Greenfield softening, so he exaggerated his boyish grin. "When have I ever let you down?" Then he held up a finger and retrieved the beehive from below deck.

Greenfield sniffed indignantly and shook her head. "The 'Star Trader', huh? Well, what's that, then? Looks like a beehive."

"It is." Baz gently handed it to the dockworker, who set it down in front of Greenfield so she could inspect it. "It's got a full brood in there. If we play our cards right, they might swarm and then we'll have two hives. Otherwise, we can go back to Narooma at the right time of year and buy a nucleus colony."

"Well, aren't you the bee expert," Greenfield said with a half-smile. "Okay, I'll find someone who can be our—what's the proper word for a beekeeper?"

"Apiarist, but beekeeper will do, I guess. That's actually something I wanted to talk to you about. Narooma has an apiarist—a good one, at that. You should see her setup. But she wants to come here and do the same thing for Flat Rock."

"Oh, she does, does she?" Greenfield asked. She rested her chin on one fist and thought. "Is she healthy?"

"From what I could see, yes."

"Does she have any other skills?"

"She built all the beehives and her apiary hut all by herself, so I guess she's good with her hands."

Greenfield looked at the beehive on Baz's trawler.

"I was thinking what it would be like to produce our own honey," Baz told her, hoping his words would play to his favour. "Then maybe we could build a meadery and diversify. I'm sure alcohol would be a great trade good we could offer to the region."

Greenfield lifted her nose. "You men and your drinks. But I have tried mead—several varieties—and

I've liked all of them. Okay, we'll do it. I'll get one of the councillors to write up a business plan for it. When this apiarist arrives, we can find a good spot to start building."

"Great, I'll make sure the next trader to Narooma will bring her back." He knelt and picked up the note plank from Narooma, giving it to Greenfield. "Here are some items Narooma needs. I said we can use them for payment for their surplus."

Greenfield frowned. "I can't wait till Ron and Anne get that paper mill working," she said, eyeing the crude timber plank with Narooma's demands scrawled onto it. "See that this order gets filled." She returned the plank and started walking away, but stopped after a few steps. "And Baz? You've done well."

"I already knew that."

This elicited a high-pitched laugh from the mayor, something few people could accomplish. "Yes, I'm glad you're a part of Flat Rock. You've done a lot for us. Star Trader . . ." Then she laughed again—a twisted, condescending cackle—and left him on the dock.

When she was out of earshot, the dockworker stepped closer to Baz and said, "You know, mate, until you got here she was in a really bad mood."

Baz spread his arms out. "Star trader *and* Saviour," he said with a cheesy grin.

CHAPTER FIVE

There were three places Baz liked to be when on Flat Rock: his house, his favourite fishing spot on East Beach, and the bar at Bayside Hotel. The hotel was a two-storey timber building by the dock wall. Visiting traders or couriers could find accommodation on the top floor, but Baz liked the bar and restaurant on the ground level. Most of the other sailors did, too.

Baz sat with his second wife, Elsa, sharing a ginger beer and bowl of salted almonds from Flat Rock's small almond orchard. The place was crammed with people—sailors, Flat Rock Guardsmen, dockworkers, farmers, tradespeople, even a few councillors—and the sound of an acoustic band drifted above the voices and clinking of recycled glass bottles.

"Did you catch the storm yesterday?" he asked Elsa.

She nodded and swallowed some ginger beer. "Sure did. It was a whopper, too. But I was just coming into Mogood Sound, so I didn't have to deal with it for too long."

"Yeah, well, I was in the middle of the bloody ocean."

"Any damage?"

"None, thankfully."

Elsa was a trader like Baz, but she moved mainly fruits and vegetables, and her main route was from Flat Rock to Mogood Bay in the southwest.

"Shame there aren't more water tanks about," Elsa said. "It would free you up a bit with your fresh water runs. Tell you what, though; you should see the ship they've built at Mogood!"

"They finished it, did they?" Baz hadn't been to Mogood for a long time, but he remembered the shell of a large ship under construction.

"It looked finished. Looks like a brig—two masts, square-rigged, and all the rest."

Baz raised his eyebrows. "They'll be able to move a lot of goods with that."

"Yeah, Greenfield better up her game or Flat Rock will fall behind in the trading sphere."

Before Baz could reply, an entourage of Guardsmen walked past the table. At their head was Captain Matt Dean. He cast a fiery look at Baz, and Baz returned the expression in kind. Matt and his men sat at a table on the other side of the bar, but were still within view.

"I still can't believe you punched him," Elsa said, shaking her head.

Baz and Matt glared at each other from across the room, their hatred searing through the laughter and music around them. "It was either me or him. He deserved it."

"I know, but he could've killed you. And he had all his cronies with him, too." She put her hand over his.

Baz smiled at her concern for him. It felt good to have someone caring about his safety. She reminded him of Mara . . .

"Here he comes," Elsa warned.

Baz looked up to see Matt approaching with two of his juniors. He suppressed a sigh and readied himself for what was to come.

"Fancy showing your face here, Baz," Matt said in his deep voice. He towered over them, but Baz stayed seated.

"I have a right to be here, Matt. I helped build this place." He tilted his head at the Guard, knowing Matt had not lifted a finger for the construction work. The Mayor's nephew had the privilege of avoiding hard work like that.

"You know what I mean," Matt replied. He rubbed the bruise under his eye. "I'm surprised Libby and James let you back in here after what you did."

"I could say the same for you, considering you started it."

"I what?" Matt barked loud enough that the music stopped.

The Captain of the Guard stepped forward and Baz rose to meet him. Matt grabbed the shorter man by the collar with both hands. But Baz's knee was ready to spring forward unseen. Some of the other Guardsmen elsewhere in the bar stood to watch the commotion.

"Matt, no!" Elsa screamed, on her feet.

"That's enough!" James called from behind the bar. He hopped over it and wiggled through the tables and chairs to the joined enemies. "Let him go. I said let him go, damn it!"

Baz saw the blaze in Matt's eyes and knew for sure that if James had not intervened, the situation would have ended a lot worse than a few nights previous.

"This isn't over," Matt told him, before releasing him with force.

"Right, the tension scale's at about ten," James said, "so I reckon you guys stay at either end of the room. Have a drink and forget about it."

"No," Baz said. "We were about to leave, anyway." He took Elsa's hand and rounded the table slowly, heart thumping.

"Running away, huh?" Matt taunted. He turned to face Baz, but James put a hand on his chest to stop him. "Get your hand off me," he growled.

As Baz made for the door, he heard the interchange behind him.

"Just take it easy, all right," James told Matt, "or I'll kick you and all your men out of here."

There was a pause before Matt replied. "Come on guys, let's have a drink."

When Baz and Elsa stepped out into the sticky night air, Baz drew his wife closer to him and they walked up the road to the Main Gate. Night shift workers busied themselves at the warehouses on the other side of the boat berths, and there were a few sailors taking care of necessary business by torchlight. The Guardsman at the gate nodded as the couple passed.

"I really wish you wouldn't antagonise him," Elsa said softly, her voice barely audible above the breeze. Thunder rumbled in the distance.

"He's just a boofhead." Baz hugged her tighter as if to reinforce his lack of concern.

The breeze made the night somewhat more pleasant than it could have been, what with the rolling storms of the season. They walked slower, Baz enjoying his time with Elsa.

"Were you always like that?" Elsa asked.

Baz chuckled. Everyone who survived the Rise felt as though they were living a second life. "No," he replied. "No, I guess I was milder. But I did defend Mara and the kids whenever I needed to."

Elsa kissed him on the cheek. "You're a good man."

They walked the rest of the short journey in silence until they reached their house—a modest building to suit basic needs and to shelter a family. As Elsa opened the door and they stepped into their privacy, the thoughts stewing in Baz's mind rolled out, thoughts he had repeated since his first fight with Matt Dean.

"I just don't understand why he had to say Suzie is dead," he seethed with his hands in the air. "Why? Why would he say that?"

"I don't know, honey. Maybe he also lost family during the Rise and he wants everyone else's family to be dead, too."

Baz shook his head, frowning.

"Then again," Elsa continued, "maybe he's just a jealous bastard who can't stand seeing your successes and freedoms."

"Ha! Freedoms. Do you mean sailing? You want to know the last time he sailed past the bay? Two years ago. Since that fiasco when he had to chase down that trader who was giving supplies to the needy . . . what's his name . . . Jeff Something. When Greenfield found out Matt fought and killed some of the people Jeff was helping, she banned him from sailing. Matt hasn't been out to sea since then. Just in the bay."

Baz and Elsa reached the shower and stripped their clothes off. It had been a few days since Baz had showered in fresh water.

"Well, whatever his reasons are for hating you, he hates you even more now because you punched his lights out last week. Don't listen to him—your daughter and your grandkids are alive. They're out there somewhere." Elsa cupped his face in her hands and kissed his lips. "I know they're out there."

"So do I," Baz said. "But they're not on Narooma."

"And I didn't see them at Mogood, either."

They stepped into the shower together, tanned bodies slick with salty sweat after the day's stormy warmth. Baz let the water run a bit harder than usual. The gravity-fed tank outside was nearly full when he checked it, and if another storm was coming it would be topped up anyway. He picked up the soap—made from pig lard—and lathered it on Elsa's back. She had great skin for her age and sun-kissed lifestyle. She sighed with pleasure as his hands massaged the soap against her back and shoulders.

"I'll find them someday," he said. "I know I will."

CHAPTER SIX

The next morning, Baz was out at the dock cleaning his trawler. Water patted against *Mara*'s hull. Baz always loved the sounds of sea life—the birds chirping, the whoosh of wind in sails, the movement of the water. He even found pleasure in cleaning his vessel, which took the better part of a day. Just like sailing, cleaning was generally a lonesome task, but he didn't mind. It allowed him to think about things, to solve the problems of the world, and to plan the next steps in his search for his family.

It was while harnessed to the very top of his mast in the late afternoon that he saw the incoming boat. He frowned—even from such a distance, it was blatantly obvious that it was another refugee boat. Its passengers crowded the single deck, the small cabin popping up in the middle of the pack. One large, tattered sail propelled them into the bay.

A solar-powered drone was already out to meet them. Baz glanced up at the observation tower and saw it was Heather Umbridge's shift. She was always trigger-happy. She piloted the drone at full speed under the midday sun, closing in on the refugee boat as it entered the ambiguous limits of the bay.

Well, Baz thought, *I might as well see what's going on.* He clambered down from the mast and grabbed his binoculars. At least this new development would break up the monotony of cleaning. He saw the faces of the refugees at the boat's bow. They waved and shouted at the approaching drone. Meanwhile, Heather blew a whistle and the on-duty Flat Rock Guardsmen rushed out from their hut near the dock and manned a purpose-built Guard catamaran as they had done dozens of times in the past. Matt Dean was among the crew.

The Guard crew left the dock in under a minute, all sails catching the breeze, moving to intercept the refugee boat. Their large catamaran, the pride of the Guard fleet, was agile, cutting through the water like some possessed beast charging its floundering prey. Baz kept his binoculars trained on them, marvelling at how well-trained the Guardsmen were and how they worked in tandem with the drone operators. Heather hoisted a red flag atop her watchtower, signalling to the Guardsmen that the uninvited refugee boat was showing no signs of turning about.

By this time, all the dockworkers had stopped what they were doing and were watching the scene unfold. Through his binoculars, Baz saw the catamaran circling the refugee boat and the drone moving in reverse, maintaining its position in front of the visitors. Voices carried over the water, adding sound to the aggressive meeting. A Guardsman was yelling at the refugees, pointing in the direction from which they came. But the refugees simply yelled back and pressed on. They were much closer now and showing no sign of slowing down. Baz had to reduce the magnification of his binoculars.

Then something made his heart skip a beat and he stood frozen on his trawler. He stopped breathing and quickly put out a hand to steady himself, while taking his eyes away from the binoculars. His heart thumped madly like it wanted to jump out of his chest. Then he looked through the binoculars again.

The sight was unchanged.

Suzie?

His lips quivered. *Is it really you?* He felt tears forming around his eyes. *Suzie?*

The short, sharp crack of a pistol brought him out of his euphoric state. The sound made him jump. It was followed by two more cracks, with small spurts of water lifting up around the refugee boat.

"Heather!" Baz roared. "Heather, don't shoot! Stop!"

"They're not turning around," Heather protested. Her curly blonde hair waved from side to side as she shook her head.

Baz lifted a stern finger at her. "You fire another shot and I'll climb up that tower and throw you out! You understand?"

That seemed to stun the girl into inactivity. Baz didn't realise how harsh he'd sounded—the words just spilt out of him. But he didn't dwell on it too long. He was already unfurling his own sails, rushing out to see if the woman with the refugees was, in fact, his daughter.

The trawler took a painfully long time to reverse out of its berth. Baz slammed a palm against the wheel, cursing the wind, which had noticeably dropped off as soon as he pulled away from the pier. But it soon whipped up again, though he had to change tack several times before arriving at the refugees. The Guardsmen held matches and glass bottles filled with flammable liquids, ready to light them up and use them to halt the refugees' progress if they continued to disobey their demands.

Baz, yelling at the top of his lungs as he approached, begged the refugees to at least furl their sails so he could speak to them. His trawler slipped between the Guard catamaran and refugees, and it was at that moment that he caught sight of the woman he saw through the binoculars. With unaided eyes, he knew without a doubt it was Suzie—the deep bond between parent and child told him so. She saw him, too.

"Dad? Dad!" She waved and shouted at him, her face a contorted mix of joy and sadness.

Baz circled the refugee boat, and Suzie pushed through the crowded deck to the other side to watch him. "I'm here, Suzie," Baz called out to her. She wiped tears from her eyes. "Don't worry. Everything will be all right."

Then a little figure crept up and stood next to her. He held on to her hand as the boat bobbed up and down. "Pop!"

"Alex!"

The Guardsmen had sailed around the refugee boat to catch up to Baz. They slowed next to him, their smaller hull gently bumping into his boat and coming to a stop.

"Will you put those damned firebombs down?" Baz barked at them.

"What are you doing here, Baz?" one of them asked with a characteristic deep voice. It was Matt Dean. "We're trying to turn this boat around."

"My family's on that boat," Baz said, pointing. "And it only took me one minute to slow them down. If I wasn't here, they would've landed by now, no thanks to you."

"Hey, mate, we've never let that happen before. We would've burnt them out of the water before they got to the island."

"Which is why I came out here. We've got to let this boat land. Look at them."

Matt looked at the refugees and snarled. "They look no different from all the others." Then he picked up a glass bottle again and addressed them. "If you lot don't leave, we're gonna torch ya!"

Loud pleas and complaints emanated from the refugees. Baz's heart sank. All they wanted was a place to live and work—Baz had seen enough struggling islands to know what his daughter must have gone through. They all looked terribly skinny, and their clothes were tattered and worn.

"I can't let you do that," Baz told him.

Matt laughed. "You what? You don't get to make that call, mate." He rubbed the bruise under his eye again.

"I know that. So bring Greenfield out here, then."

"Oh, come on, Baz. She's gonna say the same thing. When was the last time she accepted a boat of people?"

"Fine," Baz said. He felt his blood boiling. "I'll hail her myself."

Despite Matt's angry rebukes, Baz pulled out a green flag from a chest next to his boat wheel and wound it up to the top of his mainmast. He breathed a sigh of relief when Heather raised the "acknowledged" flag atop her watchtower.

Matt grumbled and faced the refugees again. "You all stay where you are. The Mayor's coming—might be your lucky day. But don't count on it. And you, Baz—" he pointed with an unlit firebomb "—I'll deal with you when we get back to land. Talking down to me in front of everyone . . ."

The Guard catamaran floated between Baz's trawler and the refugee boat, blocking Baz's view of his daughter and grandchild. Mayor Greenfield must have acted swiftly, for her private yacht was already halfway across the bay, her green and white striped standard flying high. Baz kept silent and avoided the occasional gaze of Matt Dean, not wanting to antagonise him further. Baz had no doubt the Guard officer would have torched the refugees. He had done it twice before. But not this time, Baz made sure.

Mayor Greenfield stood with her hands on her hips as her yacht crew brought the craft alongside Baz's trawler. He now had Greenfield to starboard and Matt to port—surrounded by the opposition.

"What's going on, Baz?" Greenfield asked. Her eyes narrowed, and her voice was filled with frustration. "Why are you out here?"

"Mayor Greenfield, my daughter and grandchildren are on this boat," he said matter-of-factly.

Greenfield shrugged. "And? What do you want me to do about it?"

Baz gritted his teeth. "I want us to take these people in—they can be of use to us on the island."

"Captain Dean, do any of these refugees have knowledge or skills Flat Rock needs?" She cast a judgemental eye over the refugees.

"No, Mayor," Matt replied from his catamaran.

"You lying bastard," Baz growled. "You haven't even asked them."

Matt swore at him and turned his back.

"What did your daughter do before the Rise, Baz?" Greenfield asked.

Knowing exactly where the conversation was going, Baz answered quietly and truthfully. "She managed a surfing shop."

"We don't need surfers, Baz." Then she walked to the bow of her yacht so the refugees could see her better. "You need to leave this place or we *will* sink you," she shouted at them. "You're not welcome here." Again the refugees protested the blunt rejection, but Greenfield wouldn't hear of it. "Captain Dean, escort them out of the bay. If they try to come back or land elsewhere on the island, burn them."

"Yes, Mayor!"

"Wait!" Baz yelled, and Greenfield straightened at the display of anger on Baz's face. "I'll escort them to Mogood Bay and make sure they don't come back."

Greenfield shot him a suspicious look. She folded her arms and squinted in the sun. "No, *you* will stay here. Matt, you escort them to Mogood. When you've seen them land there, come home."

With that, Greenfield ordered her yacht crew to take her back to Flat Rock, leaving Baz seething at her orders. He looked at Matt, who wore a smug face, and then at his daughter, who was just as upset as the rest of the refugees.

Matt still clung to the unlit firebomb, and Baz's mind raced with the possibilities of what Matt might do when away from Baz's scrutiny.

CHAPTER SEVEN

Baz followed Greenfield's yacht the short distance back to the dock. He was fuming with rage and more than a little anxious. How was it possible that after years of searching for his family, he was denied the reward when it just about fell into his lap?

Greenfield's yacht crew docked at the private pier reserved for the Mayor and her councillors, whereupon she disembarked and started walking through the dockyard. Baz hurried to berth his own boat and wasted no time rushing to catch up to her.

Before he could say a word, and without turning to face him, Greenfield said, "You've got some explaining to do, Baz." Then she continued on her leisurely stroll.

"My daughter and grandkids—"

"No," she said, "you listen to me first." Then, in hushed tones, she berated him as only a tyrant could. For ten minutes, she rebuked his disobedience, his carelessness, and his public opposition to her mayoral mandates. She peppered her speech with vile words, keeping her voice low as they passed the other Islanders. By the end of it, her face was red and there was a little throbbing vein in her forehead.

"Well," Greenfield grumbled at last, "what have you got to say for yourself?"

Baz sighed and clenched his teeth before responding. "My daughter and grandkids were on that boat, and I wasn't going to let your idiot nephew butcher them because of your stupid immigration policy."

"You watch your tone," she said, stopping in her tracks and pointing a finger at him. "And you leave Matt out of this."

Obviously, attacking her nephew wasn't the right way to get through to her, so Baz breathed deeply and adjusted his approach. "Did you even see the state of those refugees? They were skin and bone."

"Vermin," Greenfield said, looking away. She kept walking, and Baz hurried to be at her side again.

"Probably all diseased. You didn't touch any of them, did you? Your daughter? Huh?"

Baz scowled. "What do you think?"

She took a step to the side and made a buffer between them, eyeing him suspiciously. Baz had occasionally toyed with her fear of diseases in the past to satisfy his dislike for her and her ridiculous immigration policy.

"I don't want you to go to Mogood Bay," Greenfield told him after a moment of silence.

"Then let me bring my family here."

"I can't do that."

"Why not?"

Now it was Greenfield's turn to sigh. "Because if I let your family join Flat Rock, then I have to let everyone else's, too. You said yourself that your daughter has no needed skills to offer, so from what I can see, she will be a drain on our resources. You have no idea the sort of management we have for food and water here."

"Then I'll have to go to Mogood."

She laughed at his reasoning. "You don't get it, do you? Look around? What do you see?"

They were in the middle of town when she asked this. What he saw was a busy street of workshops and businesses. People moved goods on carts, either to the local market or down to the docks for trade. As the land rose in the distance, he could see the rooftops of houses, every one of which had been built by Flat Rock citizens in the years since the Rise. The road was stamped hard and free of grass or weeds and was in the process of being cobbled with local stones. Then there were the accomplishments he couldn't see—the bigger buildings like the lumber mill, the toolmaker's shop, the local cabinetmaker's factory, the butchery, and so on, all of which were in a separate district, and all operating without electricity.

"I see the most successful island in the South Coast," Baz replied, repeating the often-said truth.

"That's right. *The* most successful island. How do you think it got this way, Baz?" Greenfield held her arms out, seeming to welcome an answer, but her question was rhetorical. "We've planned, we've built, we've improvised, and we've invested. We have rules that ensure our success, and we have detailed plans for everyone on this island. You serve a purpose—a big purpose, I might add. You were the one who figured out how to desalinate saltwater on a sailboat. You helped Flat Rock make a name for itself, and because of that, you are closely linked to its success. Do you get what I'm saying?"

Baz knew the answer. He knew it all along. "You own me."

"Yes," she said with a smile—an evil, twisted smile. "I do own you. Flat Rock owns you. The monopoly on desalinisation is ours, and we cannot pass that technology on to another community."

"You can keep it, for all I care. I just want to be with my family."

"Don't take me for a fool, Baz." Greenfield sniffed and shook her head. "Wherever you end up, someone will want that knowledge. No, I think for the time being you'll stay put here on Flat Rock. You're banned from sailing until I let you out again."

Baz stepped out in front of her, and she stopped and lifted her chin at him, glaring in defiance. "You can't do that!" Baz said. "People need my fresh water. We can't keep up with the current demand with just one boat. We need two. You can't keep me here."

"Who said we won't be using both desal boats? You've been training up young Lachlan. I'm sure he can carry on your routes while you stay back and cool down."

Baz took a step closer to Greenfield, but she didn't flinch. "Nobody sails *Mara* but me. Nobody."

But Greenfield just stepped around him and continued walking. They left the town limits and were walking on a dirt track leading to the councillors' houses, the original houses from before the Rise. Cows grazed either side of them as Baz marched after Greenfield. A

Guardsman passed them on the road, saluting to the Mayor and shooting Baz a suspicious glance. Mayor and trader walked in silence for some time, each having said their piece.

When they reached her homestead—a lovely old house atop a verdant hill—Greenfield stopped at her front gate and regarded him with cold eyes. "Baz, if you even try to go to Mogood, I will sink you. I will sink you and your boat so deep, not even the scavenger divers from Sydney or New Wollongong will find you."

The threat stabbed him like a knife. He knew Mayor Greenfield to be an iron-fisted woman with molten metal coursing through her veins, but he had never been on the receiving end of one of her threats, let alone a death threat. She stared at him with those steely eyes as if willing him to defy her again. It was then, under Greenfield's possessed glare, that Baz realised she was deadly serious. If he went to Mogood Bay, she would kill him. There was not an ounce of doubt in his mind.

"You remember Jeff Coombs?" she asked. Baz nodded, understanding where she was going. "Jeff broke the rules, Baz. And he paid for it. There's a reason why you've never seen him again. Remember that."

She stepped through her gateway and along the garden path, apparently finished with her disobedient subject. But Baz had one more thing to say. A surge of courage coursed through his veins, and the words rolled off his tongue.

"I just want you to know," Baz started, and Greenfield turned to listen, "that I think you're the most heartless person on this island. You're an evil woman to drive a wedge between a man and his family. Maybe it's because you have no family, or maybe it's because your position has gone to your head. I don't know what happened to Mr Greenfield, or even if there was a man in your life, or if you have children or grandchildren of your own . . ."

He stepped forward and leaned on her front gate. "But what I do know is that you're an evil woman, and you'll always be alone. Someday, I'll be with my daughter and I'll have the joy of seeing my grandkids grow up. But you will have nobody. You'll be alone in this big house, an old woman with no friends or family, just work colleagues and enemies. And then one day you'll die, and they'll bury you somewhere, and, eventually, you'll be forgotten. Flat Rock will go on without you, and your stupid political and economic agenda will be no more."

He stepped back and took a deep breath, his heart racing, wondering whether he had just signed his own death warrant. Not wanting to stick around and find out, he turned and left, leaving Greenfield speechless in her garden.

Conflicting thoughts fought in Baz's head as he retraced the path back to town. One voice told him he should be grateful Greenfield hadn't immediately blown up at his rant. The other said to be wary of the woman who could maintain her cool in such a situation.

So he walked with haste, knowing his time was limited. He had to find Elsa. He had to take action.

CHAPTER EIGHT

Even eating his favourite meal for dinner did nothing to improve Baz's mood. Elsa had heard about the altercation in the bay and made sure to cook up some of the island's beef sausages and serve them with fried eggs and a healthy salad, but Baz said nothing more than a "thank you". So they ate in silence. He didn't like brooding in front of Elsa, but he needed time to cool down and mull thoughts over in his mind. Desperate times called for desperate measures.

"They took them to Mogood," he said, finally. He pushed his empty plate forward and picked up a glass of water. "I hope Matt didn't do anything to them on the way."

"He wouldn't dare," Elsa said.

"Yeah, I don't know. He had a look in his eye like he'd found my weakness." *Which he did,* Baz thought as he sipped the water.

"Well, he's been gone for six or seven hours already. I'd say he followed them all the way to Mogood without incident. Liam will look after them, now—he's a good man."

Liam Scullard was Mogood Bay's young, energetic, and popular mayor. Baz knew he was a hospitable man. He nodded and took Elsa's hands in his own. She smiled at the unexpected gesture.

"Do you remember when we were told to get married?" Baz asked her.

She closed her eyes and tried to stifle a laugh, but it escaped as a chuckle. "Yes. Greenfield was pairing everybody up."

Baz nodded again. "I don't think I've told you this before, but I was not very happy with being forced to marry nearly a complete stranger 'for the continued growth of Flat Rock'. I had recently lost Mara, and I was feeling pretty hopeless. I know we didn't really discuss our feelings when it all happened—we just got on with it. But . . . you've been such a support in my life. You've helped me through my grief, and you've made a sincere effort to love me—even when I didn't make it easy for you. Well, I've grown to love you, too. For the last six years that we've been married, you have been the only family in my life, and you've always been there for me. I have always appreciated that."

Elsa squeezed his hand, but Baz wasn't finished.

"Which is why I need to ask you something. You can refuse if you like, but I feel you deserve a choice, since the decision I've made could change your life forever in more ways than one."

Elsa tilted her head and looked into Baz's eyes. He could see her concern and her eagerness to hear what he had to say, which spurred him on.

"I'm going to make a break for Mogood—" Elsa raised her eyebrows "—but please hear me out. Greenfield cannot keep me from being with my family. I want to reunite with them, but, in doing so, I don't want to leave behind the family I've been with for the past six years. Would you be willing to come with me? To try to escape to Mogood?"

The silence at the table was only broken by the wind whistling around outside. Elsa blinked a few times, and for a second Baz thought she might reject his offer, as was her right. No Flat Rock citizen had ever left the island by choice. The threat of an ambiguous "severe punishment" had kept any thoughts of emigration at bay.

Baz saw her hesitation, saw her mind and heart being pulled side-to-side by competing loyalties. "If it helps," he said, "I've already given some thought as to how we could do it."

She squeezed his hands again. "Go on."

"You regularly go to Mogood for trade, right?"

Elsa nodded.

"When are you going next?"

"Tomorrow morning."

"Perfect. Listen—" he lowered his voice "—you go as you normally would. But don't come back. Meet up with my daughter and wait there for me to arrive. I'll come as soon as I can get out of here."

"But you're not allowed to leave the island at all," Elsa said. "How are you going to escape when everyone knows you're landbound?"

"I don't know, but I'll figure it out somehow." He fetched a writing plank and scratched a message into it—*See you soon.* "Here, give her this when you get there. And don't worry about me. I still have a few tricks up my sleeve."

Elsa took the plank and her eyes welled up. Baz felt so content with her in his life—she had truly been the rock that anchored him during the tumultuous period in his life after Mara had been killed and he lost contact with Suzie and the grandkids. And now they would part, if

59

only briefly. But worry still gnawed at Baz's mind. There was always the possibility that he would not be able to leave Flat Rock, or that he would die trying.

CHAPTER NINE

Elsa left at sunrise, saying goodbye to Baz with a parting kiss. Alone in the house, Baz was left to his own devices to dream up some way of escaping Flat Rock. After some hours frantically thinking of ideas and then throwing them aside, Baz decided to get some fresh air.

The sun was already warm when he stepped into its majestic shine. It was a welcome relief after the wet, overcast days. But leaning against a lamp post across the road was a Guardsman. His eyes were on Baz the moment the trader left the house.

A prisoner on my own island, he thought. Well, he wasn't going anywhere prohibited at the moment. What he really wanted was some time to think, so he went to the dock.

And the Guardsman followed.

The dock was busy, which was how Mayor Greenfield liked it. Baz kept out of everybody's way, taking a seat on some barrels by the dock wall. He watched the goings-on with casual interest while his mind worked in the background, trying to come up with some viable plan. The Guardsman who followed him stood with his two comrades by the gatehouse at the dock wall. There were so many boats berthed at the dock, all Baz could see were masts and rigging, all competing to be the tallest. *Mara*'s rigging was lost in the sea of timber and rope.

While considering a new plan, a young man of almost twenty approached Baz. "Morning, Skipper."

Baz swallowed his annoyance at being interrupted. "Good morning, Lachlan."

"We've got a shipment to Kiola later today, so I thought I'd get the goods loaded early."

Lachlan was a good guy—hardworking, attentive, and he took initiative. Baz knew he would make a good sailor and trader one day.

"Sorry, Lachlan, I'm banned from sailing for a bit."

"Banned?"

"Yes, banned."

Baz could see he was itching to talk about it. The younger man fidgeted and opened his mouth a few times before looking away. Baz looked away, too, waiting for him to ask the inevitable question, something he'd already asked a few times in the past.

"Can I sail to Kiola instead?"

This time, Baz smiled and shook his head. "Nobody sails *Mara* but me."

"I know, but . . ." Lachlan sighed. "This time it's different. We have an order to fill."

But Baz shook his head again. "Nope. Go and ask another merchant to do our order for us, courtesy of Mayor Greenfield's ban on Baz Cosgrove."

Lachlan's shoulders slumped. "All right."

"Sorry, mate," Baz told him. "When you have a boat of your own, it'll be different." He crossed his arms and leaned back against the dock wall, feeling its coolness on his shoulders. "See if whoever you ask will let you go with them. It'll be good experience for you."

"Okay."

"You should stop those dockworkers loading *Mara*." *Because I will need her empty for when I make a run for it.*

"Will do." Lachlan turned to obey his mentor's orders, but Baz stopped him.

63

"Hey, listen. You're a good apprentice, and I know you can sail. But *Mara* means a lot to me."

Lachlan nodded. He knew the link *Mara* had to Baz's past. "I understand." Then he trudged off.

Baz felt a bit guilty about how firmly he'd shot down his apprentice. Lachlan had worked for him for two years and had learnt just about everything to do with sailing in that short time. But it was a stormy season, and the young man had little experience sailing in violent weather. That was why Baz had left him at home when he went to Narooma, and it was also why he didn't want to entrust him with his most prized possession—the boat named after his dead wife.

The sun glinted off the water and shone directly on Baz, so he decided to fetch his wide-brimmed hat from *Mara*, since it was closer than going to his house. As he made his way down the pier where *Mara* was berthed, he heard a voice behind him, punctuated by heavy footsteps.

"Hey, where do you think you're going?"

Baz turned to see the Guardsman who'd followed him from his house.

"Trying to slip away from me, are you?"

"No, mate," Baz said grumpily. "I'm getting my hat."

"Where is it? Out in the ocean?"

"Relax, Paul. It's in my boat." By this time, Baz had made it to *Mara*, but Paul gripped his arm. "Fine, you can get it for me. It's in the deckhouse."

Paul, already sweating from doing his surveillance in the sun, looked Baz up and down before stepping over *Mara*'s gunwale. The Guardsman strutted to the deckhouse with such a flippant nonchalance that Baz had to bite his tongue. Goodness knew what the man was doing in his deckhouse, his private sanctum on the boat. When Paul emerged with the hat, he tossed it to Baz before he stepped back onto the pier.

"Thanks, mate," Baz said, donning the hat and walking briskly away, leaving Paul to stumble after him.

Baz fetched a bottle of water from a vendor in the dockyard—free, because he was the one who desalinated the stuff—and got chatting with an old man who was doing the same. Paul took up a position some distance away.

"I see what happened to you yesterday, Barry," the old man, Clem, said.

Clemente Benuzzi was universally adored on Flat Rock. A former builder and widower of many years, the old Italian man had retired to the South Coast for a fresh start in life—as fresh as fresh could be at his age, anyway. His penchant for making homemade salami, guanciale, and pancetta made him popular with the local butcher and the other Islanders who enjoyed special meats, including Baz. His mild manner could also soothe the fieriest of hearts.

"Yeah, I'm not happy about it," Baz told him.

Clem motioned him over to a wooden table with handmade chairs in the shade. "A man is no finished without his family," Clem said in a strong Italian accent.

Baz smiled. "I've known that for years."

"For me, the same."

"How do you manage?" Baz sipped his water, ready to listen. He loved listening to Clem.

"Ah, well, is no easy. I think about my Isabella all the time. She like an angel, but the cancer . . ." Clem shrugged and his eyes went glossy. "When I lose my wife, I feel like a flower with no petals. But I have the good memory." He tapped his head and chuckled, which made Baz smile. "So, your daughter is alive?"

Baz nodded sadly. "Yes. But I'm not allowed to see her."

Clem put his hand on Baz's wrist and squeezed. "Only the Devil pull people apart."

"The Devil?" Baz asked, failing to suppress a chuckle. But he let himself laugh because he supposed Mayor Greenfield was devilish, in a sense.

Clem laughed, too, apparently thinking along the same lines. "You do the right thing," he said.

A breeze whipped up, cooled by the shade under their thatched canopy, and Baz looked out at the boats again. There was a band of dark clouds on the horizon. The storms were not over yet.

Do the right thing, Baz repeated in his mind. "I will."

Clem nodded and sat back in his chair, exhaling in pleasure at the cool breeze flowing over him.

"But I'll have to watch out for *him*, first," Baz said, pointing to a man walking through the dockyard.

Clem studied the man and scoffed. "*Disgraziato.*"

Baz didn't know exactly what Clem said, but he caught the gist of it from his tone. They both eyed Matt Dean as he marched wearily along a pier and stopped at the guardhouse by the dock wall. Paul pointed to Baz, and Matt whipped his head in the trader's direction. He scowled, but then went on his way into town.

"He no good," Clem said.

"No." Baz stood. "You look after yourself, Clem."

"Always, Barry." He gave a toothy smile, pushed back the three or four white hairs on his head, and drank some water.

Somehow, the short conversation with Clem had cleared Baz's mind. He already had a good plan in the works as he returned to his house, boosted by Clem's subtle words of support.

CHAPTER TEN

Baz had a plan. He wasn't sure if it would work, but it was the best he could manage. He had to wait until Flat Rock went sleepy in the early hours of the morning, so— to pass time—he visited the Bayside Hotel.

It was loud and people were distracted with music, food, drink, and conversation. James waved at him from the bar, but apart from that, it seemed few noticed his entrance. Baz took a vacant seat by a wall and "bought" a bottle of non-alcoholic ginger beer. He satisfied his bar tabs with water, since the Bayside Hotel always needed plenty of water.

He didn't have long to sit idly by before a familiar face walked into the room, carrying two big bags. It was

Deidre from Narooma. Baz turned his head in a half-hearted attempt to hide, but out of the corner of his eye, he saw her approaching his table.

"Fancy seeing you here," Deidre said with a smile. She slumped down in a vacant chair.

"You made it," Baz said, trying to sound happy. Deep down he did feel pleased for her, but what he really wanted right now was to be left alone.

"Yes, and thank you so much for helping me get here. This place is amazing! It's so well-organised. How are my bees I gave you?"

"Mayor Greenfield found someone to manage them, and I passed on your instructions. As far as I know, they're doing fine. When did you get here?"

She pointed to her bags like it was obvious. "Just got off the boat. I was told to ask at the hotel if they had a room I could stay in."

"Yeah, there are rooms upstairs, but a lot of foreign sailors use them for overnight stays, so don't let them give you any crap." Baz considered letting her stay at his house, just so she could be more comfortable. After all, it would be vacant for good after he left. But he scratched that idea. *It might not look right if I bring a woman into the house when Elsa is away.* "You'll have to barter with James and Libby for some sort of payment—they'll give you a room here. Maybe you can set up a loan for honey.

I reckon they'd want to produce some mead to sell at the bar."

Deidre nodded slowly. "That's not a bad idea."

Baz waved for Libby to come over and when she did, she studied the new face carefully before warming to Flat Rock's new addition. They worked out some sort of accommodation and payment arrangement, close enough to what Baz suggested. Then they chatted amicably while Baz half-listened, glad that he could zone out and think about life, about Suzie and Alex being forced away from Flat Rock, and hoping Elsa made it safely to Mogood and had linked up with his family.

Libby returned to her duties, promising to help Deidre get settled in later.

"She's nice," Deidre said with a smile.

"Yeah, *most* people are here."

And as if that was his call, Matt Dean, the Captain of the Flat Rock Guard, made an entrance. He stood at the hand-crafted timber doors of the barroom, hands on hips, scanning the room. He only moved after his eyes locked with Baz's like an eagle spotting its prey. He weaved through the tables and came to Baz's side.

"Well if it ain't Flat Rock's very own rebel with a cause," Matt said with a smirk. He leaned closer and whispered hoarsely, "Heard about the ban Auntie Bev put on you." But when Baz only frowned at him, he

71

flicked his head to Deidre. "And who's this? I've never seen *you* before."

"Deidre," she said, offering her hand.

Matt didn't shake it. "You don't look like a sailor."

"I'm not. I'm an apiarist."

"What's that?"

"A beekeeper."

"I see. What are you doing here?"

Deidre cocked her head. "I live here, now."

"Oh, really?"

"Yes," Baz said firmly. "By your dear Auntie's invitation."

Matt straightened. "Well, what the Mayor wants, the Mayor gets, right?" He chuckled. "Like your little sailing ban." He laughed louder as he walked away, but Baz couldn't contain himself.

"*You* should know what it's like to be banned from sailing," Baz called without turning his head. He heard the Guard Captain's footsteps returning. "What's it feel like to sail on the ocean again, Matt?" he taunted.

Some of the nearby bar patrons quieted and listened.

"Felt good, old man," Matt said, leaning in close to Baz. "Felt real good. We had fine weather most of the way." There was a pause as Matt seemed to weigh up his next words. "Look, I didn't torch your daughter or the other filthy refugees she was sailing with. We left them at Mogood, just like Auntie Bev ordered."

Baz let out the breath he didn't realise he was holding. He didn't thank Matt aloud, but he closed his eyes and silently thanked his lucky stars instead.

"In fact," Matt continued, "since you can't go and see her, I might as well visit her myself. She did look lonely and scared . . ."

And Baz snapped. The very thought of Matt interfering with his daughter was enough to incite a father's rage. He grabbed the neck of the ginger beer bottle, and in one swift movement rose and smashed it over Matt's face. The officer cried out at the sudden attack and stepped back, hands on his bleeding forehead. Deidre screamed and pushed her chair back, stumbling in her rush to get out of the way.

Baz, now on his feet, sent a fist into Matt's gut, the taller, younger man bending at the strike. Matt moved his bloody hands to his gut and moaned in pain, and Baz took another swing at his exposed, undefended face.

A group of off-duty Guardsmen, clearly deciding that it was time to intervene, came to the defence of their commanding officer.

Two grabbed Baz by the arms while a third put a knee into his gut, pushing him backwards into a chair.

Baz lifted both his legs into the air and kicked his attackers away, but another took a swing at him. He turned his head to the side at the last moment, so that the fist lightly touched Baz's chin and only stunned him rather than knocking him senseless.

By this time, most of the men in the room were on their feet, yelling and taking sides. Uniformed Guardsmen had entered the barroom and joined the fray. Someone was bellowing for the fight to stop, but nobody paid attention. Then there was a heavy banging which caused enough pause in the fight for a calmness to spread in the room. It was James behind the bar, holding a heavy metal baseball bat he'd brought with him when he fled to Flat Rock. Libby held a solid timber one, turned and supplied by the local cabinet maker.

"Everybody shut up!" James yelled, and the last noise was silenced. He rounded the bar, gripping his baseball bat in one hand. He looked menacing with his dark apron and black beard. "I've had enough of you two," he said, pointing to Baz and Matt with the thick end of the bat. "This is at least the third time you've fought with each other. I don't want it in here anymore. So for as long as I see fit, you're banned from this place. You hear me? Banned! Now get the hell out of here and don't come back."

"And throw him in the Lockup!" Matt barked, wiping blood from his face.

A team of Guardsmen dragged Baz out of the silent room, past Deidre with her stunned face, to his confinement in the Flat Rock Prison.

CHAPTER ELEVEN

Baz sat in a pile of misery on the bed in his cell. Flat Rock Prison was constructed almost entirely out of heavy blackbutt logs, but the cosy feel of all that timber did nothing to warm Baz's mood. The Guardsman in charge of the prison that night was genuinely surprised to have a visitor in one of his cells—and the Star Trader, no less! When he'd asked Baz's escorts what the charge was, the Guardsman only grunted upon hearing that Baz had glassed their captain.

The night passed without incident. The only sound Baz heard was the Guardsman's soft snoring— perhaps he was not accustomed to staying awake to watch a prisoner. Baz would periodically creep over to the large cell door and peek through its small, square opening, checking if his warden had moved. But the lone Guardsman stayed put, asleep with his feet up, arms crossed and chin buried in his chest.

Baz could do nothing about his situation, so his mind wandered through a forest of negative thoughts. He feared for Suzie's safety, especially now that Matt Dean's sailing ban had evidently been lifted. He didn't know how long he was to be locked up, nor what punishment Greenfield had in store for him.

Hitting the Mayor's nephew . . . again! What were you thinking? Now you're stuck here! He berated himself over and over, as if repeatedly stabbing his heart would make the situation any better. *You're such an idiot. Now you'll never see—*

A soft tapping caught his attention. When Baz glanced at the cell door, he saw Deidre peering in at him, a finger over her lips. She looked behind herself and then back at Baz, holding up a hand. The Guardsman snored softly in the background. Deidre focused on the lock of the cell door. Baz heard a click and Deidre's head snapped around again, but the snoring continued. Then she looked down and continued doing what she had started. The latch squeaked just a bit too loudly for Baz's liking, but when Deidre opened the cell door he breathed a sigh of relief at seeing the Guardsman still enjoying his slumber.

It was only now that Baz noticed that Clem was also in the room, and he motioned for Baz and Deidre to follow him. He led them outside into the cold morning. A dense fog hung over the island, but Clem knew where he was going. He hushed any noise from his younger accomplices as they moved through the quiet streets, leaving the prison behind.

When they arrived at Clem's house, the old man spoke in a low voice. "You no have much time if you still want to go. There is fog everywhere, even on the bay."

Baz was still coming to terms with what they had done for him. "Thanks . . ."

"You helped me get here," Deidre said. "Now I wanted to help you. After those Guardsmen took you away, Clem came into the bar and we got talking. He told me how you weren't allowed to be with your daughter. So, this is my way of repaying your kindness."

"Deidre, you shouldn't—" Baz swallowed, thinking about the danger she had put herself in to help him. "Thank you."

She regarded him with a small smile.

"But now you need to hide. If anyone finds out you helped me escape, there's no way you'll be allowed to stay on Flat Rock. Or worse. Greenfield's getting crazier these days."

Deidre nodded, then sprung forward, giving Baz a tight hug. "Good luck, and thank you," she said, turning to go to one of Clem's back rooms.

"I say she can stay here," Clem said. "Is safer than the hotel."

Baz nodded. "How am I going to get to my boat, Clem?"

"No worries," Clem said with a grin. "It's fog outside. You hide in fog. And when you get to the dock, nobody will see you."

"How will nobody see—"

"Trust me. Nobody will see you." His grin grew wider, like he knew something Baz didn't. "Take this."

He handed Baz a hat. The conviction in the older man's voice filled Baz with courage. He shook Clem's hand, surprised by his strength.

"Thanks, Clem. I really mean it. You be careful, now."

"I will." He chuckled childishly. "I was sleeping this whole time."

Baz donned the hat and left with a smile on his face, hoping Deidre and the old man would be all right. The fog was thick—so heavy that Baz could barely see the house next to Clem's. He moved as quietly as possible on the stamped earth road, the fog parting as he sliced through it and joining again behind him.

A pair of Guardsman on a routine patrol came into view at an intersection. At first, they were dark blobs in the fog, but then they clearly materialised into a threat. Baz ducked behind a tree and watched them, his heart racing. They walked slowly through the intersection, looking up each road. Their voices carried in the cold air, and for a moment Baz thought they might travel up his road. Then a dog started barking nearby, and the Guardsmen whipped their heads in Baz's direction.

Baz swore and lowered himself even more. He could feel his heartbeat in every extremity—from his fingertips to his toes. The Guardsmen marched towards him, looking at the houses on either side of the dirt road while the dog kept barking. When they were just a few metres from his crouched position, someone shouted at the dog from one of the houses. Immediately, the barking ceased.

"You think we set it off?" one of the Guardsmen asked.

Before the other could answer, the dog barked again, only to be yelled at again by the irate Islander.

"Let's get out of here," the other Guardsman said quietly, and they retreated to the intersection where they continued in the opposite direction, patrolling the area.

Baz slipped out from his hiding place and kept moving down to the dock. His head spun at the thought of getting caught. So far, there was no mad rush of Guardsmen prowling the island looking for him, so he guessed his escape had not yet been discovered.

As he neared the dock wall, his gaze fell on the guardhouse by the gates. He crouched low behind some scrub, cursing the impenetrableness of the area. If he stayed there too long, he was sure someone would see him, and then his escape would be over just as suddenly as it began. Baz's fingers danced on his knee as his mind raced through possible alternative routes. Short of climbing over the wall or onto the roof of a warehouse, the only way to the docks was past the guardhouse. He remembered a few small timber crates on the front porch of a house he'd passed.

Maybe . . .

Pressed for time—for there was no telling exactly when the fog would clear or when his escape from the Lockup would be discovered—Baz retraced his steps to the house in question and casually picked up one of the crates. He hoped carrying a crate would make him look like a dockworker or producer bringing something for export. So, with his hat tipped low and his head bent lower, he marched forwards to the opened gateway in the dock wall, past the guardhouse. Out of the corner of his eye, he could see a Guardsman inside minding his own business. Before he turned right to go to the pier at which *Mara* was berthed, he saw another Guardsman patrolling the area near the Bayside Hotel, in the opposite direction to where he had to go.

This is it. Encouraged by such luck, he quickened his pace. Dockworkers were already pushing wagons and trolleys of goods and produce to and from merchant boats. Baz breathed deeper and faster in rhythm with his heartbeat, hoping nobody would give him a second look. He passed the little shop where he'd chatted to Clem the previous day and made a beeline down that stretch of dock, dodging and weaving around busy dockworkers entering and exiting the warehouse on his right.

When he reached the end of the path and was just about to go down *Mara's* pier, he came face to face with one of the dock supervisors. Time froze, and Baz felt the blood drain from his face.

I'm finished, he thought.

The supervisor, a young woman named Rochelle, looked him up and down, lifted her chin, and called out to the dockworkers around her. "Guys."

Baz turned, expecting some burly men to come up and drag him away. He would have given in to them, too, because there were far too many dockworkers to consider fighting and making a spectacular escape.

Instead, every worker had stopped what they were doing and turned their back to him. When Baz faced Rochelle, she had also turned around. Nobody spoke, but Baz heard their silent words as if they had been shouted from a mountaintop.

Go. Go, you fool!

His feet moved before his brain knew what was happening. He passed Rochelle and walked briskly to his trawler. *Mara* sat where he'd left her, ready to be taken out to sea. He put the crate down on the pier before freeing her from her mooring cleat—no sense stealing someone's belongings—and boarding her. As fast as he could, the sails were set and they caught the very slight breeze. *Mara* responded, moving back. He turned the wheel and took off between the lines of boats docked at the piers either side of him.

The joy of escaping on *Mara* filled Baz with such exhilaration that he had to consciously stop himself from yelling in triumph. The fog was still thick, so he was confident that no drone or watchtower Guard would witness his escape. When he was free of the piers, he added more sail and kept going faster. He knew the bay was deep and wide enough that he could sail comfortably by memory. Once he saw the bay's headlands, he had open ocean ahead and nothing in his way for the journey to Mogood.

The first thing he did once he was out in the ocean was find the tattered jumper his daughter had given him years ago. He slipped into it, smoothing it over his body and appreciating the warmth it gave his body and heart. Then he turned east to go deeper out to sea, after which he would go south to sail down the side of Flat Rock, but far enough out that he wouldn't be seen after the fog lifted.

He exhaled with relief, his heartbeat settling. "I'm coming for you, Suzie."

CHAPTER TWELVE

Pockets of blue sky appeared above Baz while he checked *Mara*'s bearing on his compass. He had been travelling south for about an hour and had maintained roughly the same speed the whole way. However, the fog necessitated the use of a chip log and compass so he knew exactly how far he had travelled.

Baz glanced down at the chip log—a bit of timber shaped like a quadrant of a circle, tied to a rope with knots spaced evenly apart. He knew the fog would clear soon, but he carried on with the task of measuring anyway. It was better safe than sorry, and it kept his mind occupied.

He threw the chip log over *Mara*'s stern like he had done countless times before. He waited thirty seconds, then counted how many knots had been pulled out to sea. As expected, he had maintained his speed reasonably well. By the time he put the chip log neatly aside, large swathes of the fog had burnt off under the sun's glare and he had to take off his daughter's worn jumper.

There was a thin, dark line of land to starboard—Flat Rock. He chuckled to himself as he thought about his escape again. *Clem. The old man was right when he said the dockworkers wouldn't see me.* He owed Clem a huge debt of gratitude. Deidre, too. Baz smiled, happy knowing that there were still some good people in the world.

It would take a few hours to reach Mogood Bay, but at least he had the whole day to get there. However, as the fog dissipated ahead of him, he noticed a different dark line on the horizon, one more ominous than land. It was another heavy band of clouds. Whether or not they were heading his way, he couldn't tell. Baz shrugged—if he had to endure some wild weather before he rendezvoused with Suzie and Elsa, then he'd gladly put up with it.

He consulted his charts. In a few hours, he'd turn west and sail between Flat Rock Island and Claybank Archipelago, directly for the northern tip of Mogood's territory. Regardless of how rough the seas became, he was determined to be in Mogood Bay before sundown, finally reunited with his family.

***

Baz performed another three-sixty degree survey of his surroundings. The waters had become significantly more choppy, and there was not an inch of blue in the sky— the whole canvass above him was grey, heavy with unreleased rain, and it had brought the wind with it. That was when he noticed the catamaran directly astern in the distance. There was only one large white catamaran that he knew of in the whole South Coast.

Baz inspected the catamaran through his binoculars. It flew the Flat Rock ensign, which was enough to make his heart race. The vessel was too far away to see who was on board, but Guard uniforms were hard to miss. He clenched his fist and swore. Then he swore again, louder, and sprung into action.

Crouched over his charts, he tried to surmise exactly where he was. He'd passed an unnamed islet barely half an hour ago. *There!* He found it on one chart, then traced a line with his finger to figure out *Mara*'s rough position. Then he calculated the distance to Mogood Bay.

Too far. I'll never make it, not with them on my tail. That cat's too fast.

Catamarans, though few and far between in the post-Rise South Coast, were faster than Baz's trawler, easier to handle in rough waters, and had a smaller risk of capsizing. Mayor Greenfield herself had commissioned this particular catamaran for the Flat Rock Guard. It said much about her twisted priorities. While Mogood Bay was building big trading vessels, Greenfield had diverted resources to construct a threatening security boat.

Baz shook his head. *And now it's after me.*

He sailed on, drumming his fingers on the chart, anxiety building within him. Greenfield said she'd have him killed if he left Flat Rock. He didn't doubt her words, and he wasn't going to let the catamaran catch up so he could know for sure.

His eyes rested on Claybank Archipelago. Good old Claybank—run by an even older retired Australian Army colonel named Stuart Renshaw—was a law unto itself. It maintained semi-peaceful relations with the surrounding communities, but only because it had a symbiotic relationship with them. Claybank's main export was bricks. And its biggest import was nearly everything else. Colonel Renshaw, whom Baz believed had more than a few screws loose, was on such shaky terms with Flat Rock that he only accepted imports from

Baz. Since Flat Rock desperately needed bricks for current and future developments, Greenfield put up with the situation, sending Baz with food and water and getting paid with the valuable building material.

But Baz had nothing to trade with Renshaw at the moment. How would the old army officer respond if Baz turned up unexpectedly, with Flat Rock Guards in tow, seeking immediate assistance, and with nothing to offer as payment?

Baz looked back at the catamaran and saw that it had gained on *Mara* faster than he'd anticipated. That made up Baz's mind. He turned *Mara* hard to port, the sails shifting at the change in direction of the gusty wind, which was now hitting *Mara* head-on. While this meant Baz's progress would be slowed—because he'd have to start tacking—it also meant the catamaran would suffer a speed and comfort deficit, too. Catamarans, by their design, had a harder time sailing into the wind. Baz hoped it would give him the necessary advantage to reach Claybank first.

As the small islands of Claybank drew closer, the catamaran narrowed the chase to within shouting distance. Baz glanced back and saw Matt Dean at the catamaran's bow, grasping a rail with both hands as his vessel bobbed and splashed in the water. His face was red with cuts and bruises after the brief bar fight.

"Where are you going, Baz?" Matt yelled.

Matt's muffled voice just reached Baz's ears. He ignored the Guard captain.

"You won't get away!"

Baz looked at the mad Guardsman and saw he held a firebomb in his hand. He was struggling to light it on the rough sea, holding onto the railing with one hand while trying to light the bomb with the other. Another Guardsman—it looked like Big Bob—came over to assist, and together they managed to light one.

Baz swore, his gaze darting back and forth between Matt and the waves around him. Matt launched the firebomb. It arced high in the sky. The wind picked up, knocking it off course, and it plummeted far off *Mara*'s stern, disappearing in the water. Baz's heart thumped and he had to squeeze *Mara*'s wheel to stop his hands shaking loose. He turned *Mara* a little to port to negotiate a wave, but this allowed the catamaran to gain on him.

At the crest of the wave, Baz checked on Matt again. The Guard vessel hit the wave on an angle just as Matt threw another firebomb. The uncomfortable angle of the catamaran's deck meant the firebomb went way off course. Baz breathed a sigh of relief as he came down the other side of the wave. The Guards' sailing error would buy him some time, but not much.

"You're a dead man, Baz!"

The relentless taunts spurred Baz on. Claybank was much closer now, so close that he could see people milling at the shorelines. They were watching and pointing at the skirmish between the Flat Rock boats. Baz checked that he had his Flat Rock standard flying high. Not that it mattered too much—his trawler was the only one of its kind plying the waters of the South Coast, the other desal boat being a converted yacht.

Baz looked behind him just in time to see a third firebomb coming his way. The bright orange flames of its cloth wick whipping madly in the air. Its trajectory was right on target.

Baz screamed profanities, freezing up with indecision. He spun the wheel unconsciously in one direction, but the incendiary weapon hit the deck behind him, smashing loudly.

He screamed again as shards of glass and cold liquid splattered his bare calves. He shook wildly at the suddenness of it all, but then he looked down at what should have been a fiery deck, only to see the flammable liquid splashed over the boards, bits of glass here and there.

The wick must have slipped out, he thought. *Or extinguished.* He sighed and willed his legs to stop shaking.

Deciding he was close enough, Baz signalled S-O-S via Morse code on his boat's lamp. Someone *had* to see it on the island. Colonel Renshaw had several methods of communicating with incoming vessels. But, just to make his point clear, Baz pulled out *Mara*'s flare gun. He aimed it skyward and pulled the trigger. The bright red flare shot upwards with a hiss, spiralling higher and higher in the wind. But there was no response from Claybank.

Another firebomb plopped into the water a few metres to starboard. Baz clenched his teeth and returned to the boat's lamp, signalling madly. He wrote: C-P-T / D-E-A-N / A-T-T-A-C-K-S. *Maybe that will get Renshaw's blood boiling.* H-E-L-P.

A few seconds later, he had his reply: R / W-C. *Roger, will comply.* Baz smiled and laughed victoriously at Renshaw's response.

The message seemed to have been communicated, because now many people were running about on the Claybank islands. Baz knew that the retired army colonel had installed all sorts of defences in his domain, and now his citizens appeared to be rushing to strategic places to 'welcome' Baz's pursuer.

Baz glanced back at Matt, surprised that the catamaran was still ploughing through the sea towards the islands. He was well aware of the skirmish breaking out last time Matt had visited Claybank, resulting in great enmity between Matt and Renshaw. Since then, Renshaw had consolidated his defences with siege weapons and fortifications. Baz wondered whether Matt would even approach the archipelago.

The Guard captain stood defiantly on the catamaran's bow, staring at Claybank. His gaze shifted to Baz, and then he yelled to the catamaran's helm: "Stay on him!" He lit another firebomb.

Mara entered the channel between two of the Claybank islands. Baz could see that the stationary siege weapons like ballistae and onagers were already manned as he entered the kill zones. The catamaran followed him into the channel and then, in a rage of sound, Renshaw's people let loose.

A storm of bricks, rocks, and metal-tipped timber bolts converged on the catamaran. Thuds and cracks mixed with the sound of shouting Guardsmen. Baz tried to turn *Mara* out of harm's way, but Matt followed. Every siege weapon to Baz's starboard side held fire, for *Mara* was too close to the catamaran for comfort. The defenders on the other side of the channel kept up the heat, firing relentlessly into the Guard boat.

Matt took shelter in the catamaran's cabin. "Baz!" he growled, along with a string of profanities.

Baz pressed on between the two islands, making sure to run the full gauntlet. Three or four bricks splashed in the water in front of him from a wayward catapult. Another brick bounced off *Mara*'s bow, while a deadly bolt ricocheted off one of the catamaran's hulls and careened across Baz's field of vision. His heart pounded at the intensity of the fight, marvelling at how Colonel Renshaw had built up his defences in only a few years.

Another bolt tore through the catamaran's tall mainsail, passing over Baz's vessel and lodging itself into a grass embankment on the opposite island. Then the catamaran careened into *Mara*, nipping the trawler's stern. The weight of Matt's boat pushed *Mara* along for a few metres, Baz fighting desperately to protect his vessel from further damage and the threat of capsizing. The sound of the bricks colliding with the catamaran was deafening. After a moment of uncertainty, the two boats came unstuck and *Mara* carried on out of harm's way.

This opened up the opportunity for the eastern siege weapons to rain hell on the catamaran. The boat was very close to the eastern island, so the force of the projectiles from that side did even more damage. To retaliate, Matt and the Guards threw firebombs up into the defensive emplacements that were within reach. A moment later, two wooden siege weapons were roaring with fire, which only fuelled the ire of the Claybank residents. Baz left the carnage behind, sailing on unhindered through the rest of the channel. He waved his thanks to the defenders watching on, and they cheered his escape.

But Matt Dean wasn't finished. He brought the catamaran to the middle of the channel again and powered headlong through the onslaught. Baz could hear the splashing of projectiles in water, the thumps and cracks when they hit their mark, and the wondrous whooshing sound of all that deadly matter flying through the air.

Baz damned the speed and strength—and possibly stubborn luck—of the catamaran, for it was on his stern again. They had reached the end of the channel, and the sea was opening up beyond. Baz decided to lead Matt through another of the archipelago's channels, because the catamaran clearly wasn't wrecked yet. Just then, he saw four Claybank boats to starboard sailing towards his position, so he turned to meet them. And stupidly, arrogantly, Matt Dean followed.

The Claybank vessels parted, allowing Baz to slip between them. Then he watched as they enveloped the pursuing catamaran, joining the fray now that the siege weapons were out of range. Matt took evasive manoeuvres, but the defenders hemmed him in. The Claybank sailors had bows, and they trained them on the

Guardsmen, yelling at them to halt their boat. Baz heard the defiant reply, then saw one of the Guards light up a firebomb and toss it at a Claybank boat. It erupted into flames, and the response was swift.

Baz looked away, not wanting to see the death that would surely come to the Guardsmen—deaths he knew he had instigated, but never wished for. His stomach felt empty at the thought, the guilt churning in him that he was driven to such lengths to reunite with his family. He wanted to say the blood was on Mayor Greenfield's hands—and in a way it was—but it was his fault too. But he'd never forget the violence he encouraged at Claybank that day. All he'd wanted was the catamaran disabled, but Claybank's retribution was likely to be much more serious than that.

And so Baz left the Guard catamaran behind him, never looking back, sailing his wounded trawler the rest of the way to Mogood Bay.

CHAPTER THIRTEEN

The sun was beginning to set when Baz approached Mogood's territorial waters, and a feeling of calm washed over him that he hadn't felt in a long time. To arrive freely without pursuers surely meant Baz was finally loose of Mayor Greenfield's iron grip.

Mogood Sound was a narrow channel on approach to Mogood Bay, and in it Baz found relief from the choppy sea. He passed another boat on its way out and returned the friendly wave offered by its skipper. Further in, the dual beacons on the opposing headlands of Mogood Bay were just being lit, giving Baz extra light as he passed into the wider waters of the bay itself.

When he turned *Mara* into the bay, he saw the tall ship that Elsa had spoken highly of. It was easily the largest vessel in the South Coast—really, it was the only vessel that could rightly be called a ship. Baz figured it could carry all the cargo of all the Flat Rock traders combined and still have room for more. It seemed Mayor Scullard of Mogood had big plans.

But Baz wouldn't be around long enough to see Mogood expand. No, Baz was determined to flee inland with his family, leaving the South Coast, Flat Rock, and Mayor Greenfield far behind.

He berthed at Mogood Dock, which was just as large and nearly as busy as the dock at Flat Rock. A dock supervisor approached to officially sign him in.

"I'm here to see Suzie Cosgrove," Baz told the man.

The supervisor smiled softly. "We've been expecting you, Baz." Then he assigned a dockworker to lead Baz straight to his daughter.

Baz's stomach clenched with a combination of nerves and excitement as they trekked uphill on wide paths winding around blackbutt trees. They passed cabins where the local, permanent residents lived, before they reached the transient section. This was where refugees and travellers were allotted temporary accommodation. Mogood was the main thoroughfare for people moving in and out of the South Coast and, because of this, the transient section was a vast expanse of tents and rough shelters.

The dockworker quickly found Suzie's tent. She emerged, shielding her face from the light and heat of the dockworker's torch. Then she realised who else was there. Her eyes went wide, she let out a cry of joy, and she wrapped her arms around her father's neck for this first time in six or seven years.

"I'm here," Baz told her, tears welling up in his eyes. "I'm here for good."

Suzie cried. While they hugged, Elsa and Alex came out of the tent. Alex shouted in surprise as he ran up to Baz, joining in the hug. Elsa stood back, smiling, letting Baz enjoy the long-awaited moment with his only remaining family. But Baz wouldn't have it like that. Recognising the new door he was opening in his life, he gestured for her to join in the hug. They became one as a family. Their lips met briefly, and he saw the joy on her face. He whispered words of thanks and appreciation into her ear.

"Where's Beckie?" Baz asked. He felt Suzie's grip tighten.

"She died three months ago, Dad," Suzie said quietly, sniffling. "Something in our food . . ."

Baz swallowed hard, but his emotions got the better of him. The dockworker dropped his head respectfully as the Cosgrove family grieved. When father and daughter finally pulled apart, the waiting man cleared his throat.

"Would you like me to tell the Mayor that you're here, Mr Cosgrove?"

Baz took a deep breath, clearing his sorrow. He nodded, and the dockworker scurried off. Since the dusk was fast turning into night and the wind was getting wilder, Baz suggested they go inside the tent. He hoped they didn't have to stay long in Mogood to ride out more storms. They sat in the cramped tent and, while Suzie wiped tears from her eyes, Baz gazed upon his daughter—the first real opportunity he'd had in years.

"So," Baz started, "where have you been all this time? I've looked everywhere for you."

Suzie sighed. "We were on the new coast somewhere near Milton."

"But that's only fifty kilometres away," Baz said, gobsmacked. "Were you there the whole time?"

Suzie nodded. "We were trying to survive there," she said. "But the land was bushy and we had no idea exactly where we were. We sent people out to try and find roads or towns further inland, but none of them ever returned. In the end, we stopped sending people because we needed all the help we could get in growing food and building our settlement."

"Didn't . . . didn't any boats come to get you? Did anyone . . . couldn't anyone find you there?" It seemed unfathomable to him, so unfair that his daughter had been so close to him all these years.

"The best land was a bit off the coast through some trees, so nobody could have seen the settlement from the ocean. We saw a few sails, but they were too far out, I guess."

"And Beckie? Did she . . . was she . . ."

Suzie put her hand on Baz's arm. "The food was killing us. There was some kind of bacteria making us sick. Beckie . . . got sick."

Alex sniffed, so Baz put his arm around him. "I'm sorry I couldn't find you sooner." He hung his head low.

"Don't be sorry, Dad. From what Elsa told us, you did all you could."

"I can't believe you were so close to me the whole time."

Suzie said nothing. Instead, she just leaned forward and hugged Baz again. His heart settled. At least now he was with her and Alex for good. Beckie's loss opened a hole in his heart right next to the one made by Mara's passing. But Suzie didn't want to talk about it, so they talked more about her settlement, how they tried to make it liveable, and how it had slowly failed.

"We left it all behind," Suzie said. "Many died while we were there. When we decided to leave, some moved inland, but most of us took to the waters. We used the same boat that had ferried all of us to the settlement in the beginning, and the first place we found after we left was Flat Rock."

"Only how were you to know Flat Rock wouldn't accept you?" Elsa said.

"Exactly. When that drone started shooting at us, I thought we were all goners. And then that idiot in the boat threatened to burn us to death."

"Matt Dean," Baz said flatly. "He won't be bothering us again."

He recounted his escape from Flat Rock, starting with his attack on Matt in the Bayside Hotel. Elsa shook her head knowingly at his irrational attack, but he ignored her and kept telling the story. He told them of his escape from Flat Rock Prison, sailing in the fog, and then Matt Dean's pursuit, culminating in the ferocious fight at Claybank.

"That Colonel Renshaw is crazier than Greenfield," Elsa mused. "Do you reckon he killed them?"

Baz grunted and spoke regretfully. "More than likely."

"Well, it was either him or you."

Baz frowned, but silently agreed with her. Just as he was about to speak, someone approached the tent.

"Susan?" The voice was familiar to Baz, but he couldn't quite put a face to it.

"It's Liam," Elsa said. She opened the tent, and Liam stepped inside and knelt down, which further crowded the interior.

Liam Scullard, Mogood Bay's mayor, shook Baz's hand like an old friend, though they hadn't seen each other for quite some time. "Good to see you made it here in one piece."

"Yeah, barely."

Liam sighed. "Look, Baz, I know your situation. I think it'll be best if I destroy your boat. Elsa's too. It's the only way to hide the fact that you came here."

Baz understood the predicament he'd put Liam in. There was no telling how Greenfield would react if she ever found out that Mogood was harbouring two fugitives from Flat Rock.

"Well," Baz started, "have any other Flat Rock traders been here since Elsa arrived?"

"Not to my knowledge."

"Okay, here's what you can do. Destroy Elsa's boat, but keep mine hidden. If Mayor Greenfield decides to punish you because, *somehow*, Barry and Elsa Cosgrove disappeared and Suzie and Alex Cosgrove are no longer at Mogood, then at least you'll still have a good source of fresh water."

"You reckon she'll cut us off?"

"I don't know. Maybe. She might do it without evidence, but it'd be foolish. Flat Rock gets a lot of supplies from Mogood. Just be prepared for all possibilities is all I'm saying."

"I understand. I'll burn Elsa's in the morning and move yours to the boatyard." He paused. "You look half-dead, mate."

Liam's aide stood outside the tent, and his torch cast a glow on Baz's face. It had been a rough night in Flat Rock Prison and an eventful journey to Mogood. A solid sleep was just what he needed.

"We'll get a good night's sleep and then we'll go. I'm sorry, but I don't think we should stay here too long."

"I understand," Liam replied. "But that's if the weather permits it. Looks like another storm is on the way."

They briefly discussed supplies needed for a journey inland at least as far as Tarago, a rapidly growing country town. Liam said they could take the train from

Tarago north or south to one of the bigger inland cities, if that tickled their fancy—if the train was still running. But they also worked out contingencies if a storm did hold them in Mogood temporarily. Then Liam bade them farewell and goodnight, promising to have their supplies ready the next morning.

"He's a good man," Baz said after Suzie zipped up the tent.

"He's been very kind to us," Suzie told her father. "He doesn't like how your mayor runs things."

"No, and I don't either. But we don't have to worry about that anymore. Come on, let's have a bite to eat and then we'll get some sleep. We have a big day tomorrow."

They ate a small meal of fruit and vegetables. Baz liked watching Alex wolf down his food like he'd never seen it before. The years spent in the bush must have been rough on him, especially after losing his sister.

After a little more chitchat, the wind picked up even more and became so loud it was hard to hear each other's words. The tent rippled and shook with each gust. They unanimously decided to turn in for the night.

Alex went to sleep next to his mother, while Baz and Elsa shared the other sleeping bag. At first, Baz was a little annoyed that he'd forgotten his holey jumper on *Mara*, but the warmth of Elsa's body soon made him forget it. They lay on their sides, with his arm over her, and she hugged his hand close to her chest like she wanted to keep him there forever. Baz didn't have much time to ponder the peace and satisfaction he felt, because in no time at all he had fallen asleep with the sound of the growing wind entering his dreams.

CHAPTER FOURTEEN

Baz awoke to the sound of soft rain as it pattered on the tent's canvas. It seemed he was the first to do so. He spent the first few minutes of wakefulness gazing peacefully at his family as they lay sleeping. But his moment of calm was short-lived as he heard footsteps outside.

"Baz? Baz?" It was Liam.

Baz stirred and woke Elsa as he moved. He opened the tent while crouched on his knees. "Come to see us off, eh?" Baz asked.

But Liam's face was downcast. "Look, Baz, there's a guy in the bay who's asking for you. He was here a few days ago when your daughter came from Flat Rock. Calls himself Dean."

"Dean?" Blood drained from Baz's face at the mention of the name. *Matt Dean. How is he still alive?* The question raced through his mind over and over again before he spoke. "What do you think we should do?"

Elsa crawled up behind Baz and gripped his arm.

"He said he'll burn our new ship if we don't hand you both over to him. He's already set fire to both of your boats."

Baz clenched his fists and exchanged a glance with Elsa, imagining *Mara* slick with flames. Then he made up his mind. *The man doesn't give up. He just doesn't give up! He's like a bloody cockroach!* He looked over at Suzie, who was propped up on one elbow in her sleeping bag. "Sweetie—you, Alex, and Elsa will make the trip without me."

"No—" Suzie started.

"He wants both of you," Liam reminded him, pointing to Baz and Elsa. "Look, I don't like this any more than you. Greenfield's gone too far this time, but I can't put my people's future and lives at risk. If he burns our ship, he might burn the dock, and that'll make things a lot harder around here."

"I know, I know," Baz said with a quick nod. "And I don't want to put you in danger. He's a loose cannon, but I still don't know why he wants Elsa, too."

Elsa squeezed his arm. "If they take you, I'm going, too."

"No," Baz replied automatically.

"Yes." She stood her ground, stared Baz in the eyes, and stayed that way until he bowed his head in acquiescence. It was something he always admired about her—that steely resolve, which he sometimes called "stubbornness", that kept her focused on the important matters. He hugged her and then turned to Liam.

"We'll be down at the dock in a minute," Baz said.

Liam nodded. "I'll see you there. Please don't be too long. But don't worry, I'm not leaving you totally in the lurch."

As Liam left, Baz saw wisps of black smoke through the trees in the direction of the bay.

When Baz looked back at Suzie, she had tears flowing down her cheeks. Alex was the same. He put his hands on their shoulders.

"Don't worry," he said. "I'll catch up to you. Wherever you go, leave notes or directions for me so I can find you. And try to travel in a group so you're not alone. Okay?"

109

Suzie only nodded, her lips still quivering with sadness.

"I love you," Baz told her, then moved into a warm hug. He could feel his daughter not wanting to let go. He spread an arm out and pulled Alex in, too. "I'll see you again. I promise."

Baz's heart felt like it had been ripped in two at the turn of events. Alex was clearly trying to be strong, but his cheeks were wet with sadness. Baz squeezed the boy more firmly. Since the Rise, his whole life had gone from bad to worse. Now there was yet another obstacle to overcome before little Alex's life would bear some semblance of normality in this new world. Baz wished them a safe journey, hugged them once more, and reiterated his promise of reuniting.

Then Baz and Elsa walked to the dock in silence, towards burning boats and a madman waiting to murder them.

***

The two vessels were roaring with fire when Baz and Elsa made it to the dock. There was so much smoke and flame that Baz couldn't even recognise *Mara*. His beautiful boat, named after his dead wife, was crumbling under the fire's raging heat. Elsa's boat, more fragile, was nearly completely consumed. Dockworkers and sailors had pushed the vessels out into the bay to keep the fires away from other boats and the heavily combustible timber dock. Their timber poles with blackened tips were evidence of their efforts, and parts of the piers where Baz and Elsa's boats were berthed had charred surfaces. The light rain was of little help, but fortunately the wind had died down.

"There he is!" Matt exclaimed to his fellow Guardsmen when he spotted the fugitives. His uniform was torn and bloodstained. "Surprised to see me?" When Baz didn't reply, the brute went on. "Thought you could finish me at Claybank, huh? Well, all you did was sink my catamaran and get Big Bob killed."

Matt stood on one of Claybank's keelboats. Its hull was marked and its sails slightly torn after the fight at the archipelago. Baz tried not to imagine the intense fight Matt would have had in order to change vessels and flee with his life.

"So now it's time you met your punishment, Baz," Matt continued. "And you, too, Elsa."

"No, they won't," Liam said. "One of my boats will take them to Flat Rock, where they will be tried, as is the decent thing to do."

"And who are you to tell me how to work this out?" Matt asked.

111

"I am Mayor Liam Scullard, and since you're in my territory, you *will* do as I say. Baz and Elsa will be transported to Flat Rock."

Matt didn't reply. Instead, he took a deep breath and shifted his position at the bow of the keelboat.

"Then it's settled," Liam continued. "I'll organise some transport, and then you can be on your way."

Matt waved a hand dismissively and went to sit with the rest of his crew—at least, those who had survived the frenzied attack at Claybank.

"I don't know what you did to cause all this," Liam said quietly to Baz, "but the least I can do is make sure you get back to Flat Rock safely."

Baz thanked him and shook his hand. The mayor wasted no time organising the new brig's crew for a voyage, and Baz, despite his sullen feelings, smirked. They would sail into Flat Rock Bay in a huge brig while their Flat Rock Guard escort, under the command of Captain Matt Dean, would be alongside them in a puny, battered keelboat from a different community. What a display that would be!

When all was ready, Baz shook Liam's hand again. "If my daughter stays here, please look after her until I return."

"Of course. You plan on coming back?" Liam asked with a grin.

Baz sighed and frowned. "Yes." But he didn't believe his own words. Then he looked at Elsa. "We'll figure something out."

She nodded, looking hopeful.

Baz and Elsa boarded the large Mogood vessel, which was aptly named *Saviour*, and stayed out of the way while her small crew of about fifteen prepared the ship for her voyage. Baz was awestruck by the beauty of the brig—it was truly a marvel of old-style shipbuilding, yet somewhat anachronistic in the modern era. He enjoyed the scene so much that he nearly forgot why he was on board in the first place. But before too long, *Saviour* was underway, moving her weight through the bay with agility and remarkable stability.

The burning wrecks of the Flat Rock vessels were the last thing Baz saw of the bay before *Saviour* slipped into Mogood Sound, where she sailed smoothly at a leisurely pace. Matt Dean and his crew followed in the keelboat. When they were out into the ocean, *Saviour*'s captain, Theo, ordered full sail and the crew obeyed. Halyards moved and sails unfurled along spars until all square and triangular sails were open and catching the wind. Then *Saviour* picked up speed, leaving the little keelboat behind before slowing down somewhat so the two vessels could travel together.

Once on the open sea, Baz looked out at the expanse of water, at the smoke still rising from Mogood, and cursed how the tables had turned. He had thought he was finally free. But now he was being taken back to Flat Rock, bound for retribution. And this time, he was certain they wouldn't let him walk away so easily.

CHAPTER FIFTEEN

Saviour pushed into Flat Rock Bay. Her size compared to every other boat demanded everyone's attention, and Baz loved every moment of it. All the dockworkers stopped and stared. Any boat plying the waters of the bay gave *Saviour* plenty of room—it truly was an exciting way for two fugitives to make an entrance.

Matt Dean's keelboat made for the Guard Boathouse off to the side of the dock, but *Saviour* had to moor in the bay. There was simply no room for her to berth at one of the busy piers. Captain Theo had his crew lower a gig into the water and rowed Baz and Elsa ashore.

When Baz stepped onto the land he thought he'd left forever, he came face to face with Mayor Greenfield.

She stood in the wind and light rain beside the dock wall, under an umbrella held by one of the many Guardsmen clustered around her. Her eyes bled hatred and her expression spoke of the betrayal she no doubt felt upon seeing him.

Captain Theo stepped forward. "Mayor Greenfield, I convey these fugitives to you, as demanded by my Mayor Scullard."

Greenfield turned to face the Mogood captain, but she said nothing to him. Standing in the rain, holding Elsa's hand, Baz felt the tension in the air like the humidity of a tropical day.

"Scullard insisted on carrying them here," Matt Dean said, approaching Greenfield from the Guard Boathouse.

Greenfield pressed her lips together tightly and stared at Baz. Then she spoke to her security detail. "Take them to the Lockup."

The Guardsmen around her pressed forward and seized Baz and Elsa.

When Theo looked as if he was going to protest, Baz shook his head and mouthed, "Thank you," before being whisked away. As he was pulled past the dock wall, Baz heard Matt Dean order Captain Theo to leave.

The Guardsmen threw the fugitives into the cool, damp cell from which Baz had escaped over twenty-four hours ago. The door latch slammed shut, and Elsa regarded her husband with a worried face. He hugged her, and she buried her head in his shoulder. Spits of rain hit him through a high, narrow window in the cell. When he looked out, he saw the blanket of grey cloud in the sky and hoped Suzie had stayed in Mogood. He didn't want her trekking through the Bimberamala National Park and up the Kings Highway in the storm.

To hide from the rain dripping into the cell, Baz and Elsa moved the single bed to a dry spot and sat with their backs against the thick timber wall. They said nothing. He could think of nothing to say; he just stroked Elsa's hair and stared at the opposite wall. Last time he was in the same predicament, Deidre and Old Clem had come to his rescue. He doubted that would happen again.

Sometime later, he heard a chair scraping outside his cell and footsteps on the stone floor. Greenfield's stern face appeared, framed by the hole in the cell door, and a rumble of thunder pre-empted her speech.

"How is she, Baz?" Greenfield asked softly, slowly. "Your daughter—how is she?"

"Safe and healthy," he growled. "No thanks to you."

"Don't be angry, Baz. You knew what the rules were." She traced the edges of the hole with a shaky

117

finger, her eyes glazed over. "And now you must pay the price."

Baz didn't bother replying. There was no reasoning with the woman.

"My nephew has told me of your exploits—how you led him to Claybank, how he had to fight for his life just to catch you. Because of you, a Flat Rock Guardsman is dead. Because of you, a Guard catamaran—the prize of our fleet—was taken by Claybank. Because of you, one trading boat and one desal vessel are destroyed. And, because of you, Flat Rock is now on very shaky terms with the other two largest communities in the South Coast." She sighed heavily. "Baz, you have done so much more than lose a water trader for Flat Rock."

"Screw Flat Rock."

"What?" Greenfield's louder voice filled the cell.

"I said, 'Screw Flat Rock'."

"I say screw it, too," Elsa said. She put her arm around Baz and pulled him close.

Greenfield shook her head and spoke quietly again. "Tomorrow you will be taken to the gallows. The rules must be enforced."

She left them without another word. As Baz heard her footsteps shuffling out of the prison, the Guardsman on duty came over and frowned at them. It was Paul, the one who had followed Baz around the day he spoke to Clem at the dock. Paul's frown was apologetic. The man's eyes spoke of his regret for Baz and Elsa's situation. Of course, he couldn't voice those feelings or act on them, or Greenfield would throw him into a cell, too. The power was twisting her mind beyond reason.

Paul cleared his throat. "Lunch will be here soon."

A flash of lightning illuminated Paul's face before he left them alone. Elsa put her head on Baz's shoulder as the thunder rolled in, and Baz put his arms around her, giving her warmth and emotional support. He felt a chill and wished for his old jumper, but then remembered it had burned along with *Mara*. As he closed his eyes, he thought of how much he hated Matt Dean. Then his mind drifted to the rope noose that awaited him the next day.

CHAPTER SIXTEEN

Later that night, a terrific clap of thunder roused Baz from his sleep. It rattled his bones as it rumbled on—one of those long, echoing episodes. The lightning also lingered, flickering for seconds, followed by another boom. That second one woke Elsa—though Baz wondered how she had managed to sleep through the first.

As Baz blinked away the sleep, he saw a faint orange glow against the wall opposite the bed. His half-conscious mind thought it strange that the morning sun should be shining when it was storming so badly. But as the cogs in his brain got moving, he knew something wasn't right. His body cracked and groaned as he sat up.

He stood on the bed to look through the window while Elsa grabbed the single sheet and brought it back to her body.

Then his eyes went wide as his face was bathed in the light of a huge bushfire not far from the Lockup. He swore, quietly at first, then repeated it louder.

"What's—" Elsa began.

"It's a fire. I think the lightning started it. Hey, Paul! Fire!" He jumped off the bed and darted to the cell door. "Fire!"

Paul got up from his chair and looked through the cell at the high window above the bed. He swore, too, and ran outside.

"Paul! Damn it, Paul, come back!" Baz pounded on the door. "Let us out!"

Elsa was trying to see out the window, but she was too short, so Baz gave her a lift.

"Oh, my goodness, look at it. We're trapped!" She fell out of his hands and got off the bed, holding him.

"We've got to get out of here." He tried lifting the bed, thinking that he might bash the door open, but it was too heavy for him alone, and even with Elsa holding one side it was too cumbersome to use as a battering ram.

"Do you think you can get out up there?" Baz asked, pointing to the window.

121

"I don't know. It's a bit small." She put her hands on her hips.

Baz didn't go there. "Come on. We've got to try."

They stood on the bed and he hoisted her up. Reaching the window sill was fine, and pulling herself up was achievable, although somewhat of a struggle. But no matter what she tried, her shoulders wouldn't fit through.

"Try and wiggle," Baz encouraged. "Try different angles."

"I am! I don't fit." Her voice was laced with panic. Still gripping onto the window sill, she stared outside and gasped. "It's getting bigger. And it's closer! There's a building already on fire over there. I think it's the logging mill."

There was impatient stomping on the stone floor and Paul reappeared at the cell door. "Come on, guys, quick."

Baz breathed a sigh of relief as Paul's keys rattled in the door. "It's already reached the outskirts of the industrial sector," he said, flinging the door open.

Outside the Lockup, the scene was chaotic. The bushfire was truly ablaze. Huge flames licked up into the night sky, which flashed all too frequently with lightning. It seemed the winds were pushing the fire in every direction. Islanders ran with buckets of water, a team of Guardsmen rushed along in a horse-drawn wagon with a tank of water, ready to hand-pump it onto the fire. Families fled to the centre of town, their children screaming. Dogs barked, and a variety of household animals were led or carried to safety.

Baz felt Elsa's grip tighten on his hand. She looked like she wanted to run, and he couldn't blame her. There was some inclination of that in his own mind—it was the perfect opportunity to flee and escape execution. But something else told him he needed to stay and fight. He still had friends on the island. If they lost their lives in the fire, Baz would forever blame himself. He *had to* help.

***

There's not enough water. That was something Baz couldn't fathom. How was it possible that in a world where the oceans had flooded whole cities, there was not enough water to fight a bushfire? His exasperation grew with each step he took in retreat from the growing blaze. In fact, it was no longer just a threat to the island town—it was already upon it, consuming the buildings like an insatiable beast. Lightning flashed frequently, as if reminding every resident of the cause of their turmoil. And the pithy rain showers coming down every so often did nothing to lighten the burden.

123

Baz witnessed the whole north-western suburb succumb to the fire's raging progress. Those houses had been built with the new bricks from Claybank Archipelago, but their strength meant nothing to nature's ferocious power. Baz's own house was older, having been constructed solely out of timber, mud, and thatching. If the fire reached his area of Flat Rock, then all would be lost.

The Islanders had given up trying to fight fire with water. The hand pumps and hoses from the fire wagons weren't enough, and passing buckets from person-to-person was laughable as well as a waste of manpower. One bright woman decided it would be better to cut a break in the fire's path to deprive it of fuel, so everyone got to work.

Baz had not worked harder or faster in his life. His arms ached with every swing of his mattock. Beads of sweat ran down his face, and his mind constantly screamed at him to flee. There was destruction everywhere he looked, and the pragmatist in him said that the island was already lost. Someone called to fall back to a safer position, and he automatically obeyed.

A team of horses neighed loudly behind him. He had just enough time to jump out of the way before they barrelled past him, pulling a wagon towards the centre of town. Mayor Greenfield sat in the bouncing wagon, wrapped in a blanket. Baz spared one glance at her house and saw it was totally ablaze. He didn't spare it a thought.

The wind pushed the fire so quickly that Baz and the other Islanders retreated even further before they had a chance to dig at their new spot. Less than half an hour later, the fire reached Baz's house. There was absolutely nothing he could do to save it or the neighbouring properties. The flames took to the wooden structures, and seemed to roar more intensely and give off even more heat—if that was possible. Baz's cheeks were burning and his eyes went watery at the harsh temperatures assaulting his face. He and Elsa clasped hands and ran, just ran, for there was nothing more to be done. Once his neighbourhood was destroyed, it was only the main avenue to the docks left. Then there was nowhere else to go.

Baz's thoughts quickly moved to evacuation. A lingering gust of wind pushed him along, and he knew only too well that the same gust would have moved the fire to the next batch of houses, encouraging it on its relentless advance. *We need to start evacuating. Now!*

There was no clear authority around him. The island councillors were nowhere to be seen, and the inadequately prepared and ill-equipped Guardsmen were just as defeated as the Islanders. Everyone seemed to be shouting at someone else or screaming in fear or pain.

Some called for their friends and relatives, and Baz hoped and prayed that their calls would be answered—the scene was already bad enough without fiery deaths added to the mix. But that's exactly what would happen if they didn't leave soon. He took it upon himself to take the lead.

"Guards!" Baz yelled. "Guards! To me!" He waved for any within sight and earshot to come closer. Paul was one in the circle that gathered around him, gesturing for others to join him. Baz told them to get everyone to the docks. If any of them were unhappy about a civilian telling them what to do, none showed it, but Baz would've been damned if he'd let a Guardsman impede any evacuation at that point in the disaster.

Once the Guardsmen had dispersed, Baz again took Elsa by the hand and pulled her along with him down to the docks. She was frightened—damn, Baz was, too!—and that fear made her slow down and stare helplessly at the carnage and desperation around her.

"Come on," Baz grunted, pulling her along faster.

When Baz and Elsa made it to the dock, they were met by the most terrifying and ironic discovery— there were only four boats moored at the piers. Baz kicked a pile of empty wooden crates stacked up near him and cursed loudly at his misfortune. Flat Rock, the South Coast's most prosperous settlement, built on maritime trade and possessing a fleet of nearly thirty vessels, now had nearly zero means of escape. The only vessels available were one dilapidated trader, the Claybank keelboat, and two purpose-built Guard ketches.

"Damn it," Baz said, clenching his fists.

Elsa laid a hand on his arm. "If most of the traders are gone, it means they are safe."

Baz nodded, squeezing her hand. It also meant that some people—Guardsmen and civilians—must have already fled, which was cowardly and selfish, unless they filled their boats with other fleeing souls. "It also means there's no way everyone can be evacuated before the fire reaches the dock."

Already, embers were falling on the damp boards, and Baz stamped one out.

"Look," Elsa said, pointing out to sea.

Baz followed her gaze. At the outskirts of the bay was Greenfield's yacht, surrounded by half a dozen other vessels. *They left us! Those bloody bastards left us!* Baz glared at the distant boats, not wanting to think of how much spare room they would've had on board.

There was a clatter of footsteps on the pier. "What's going on?" Paul asked between pants.

"There goes our Mayor and councillors, and who knows who else," Baz said with an angry wave of the hand.

127

He looked in the direction that Paul had come from. A flood of townsfolk were already rushing down to the apparent safety of the dock. The sound of crying babies and children pierced Baz's eardrums. Too many people shot too many questions his way—foremost among them were various versions of: "Where the hell are all the boats?"

As more and more people crowded the piers, Baz found himself being pushed by the growing crowd. His hand slipped from Elsa's, but she was quick to yell and push her way back to his side. Lightning flashed and thunder cracked, eliciting fearful shouts from the crowd.

Nobody was acting sanely. Some boarded the few boats left in the dock, only to be chastised by a few righteous Guardsmen. The failed escapees were yanked off the gangways while Paul climbed the mast of one boat so he could be seen by all.

"The women, children, and elderly can board and get out of here!" Paul yelled above the clamour.

"No!" came an anonymous voice from the crowd. "Not the elderly. The younger ones should go instead."

"I can't find my husband!"

"Mummy?"

"Get out of my way! Move!"

Once again the crowd descended into a frenzy of yelling and stampeding, while the sky burned with a terrible orange glow. Too many people rushed onto the vacant boats. One of the gangways snapped, and Baz heard terrified shouts as people fell between the pier and the boat. Recovery ropes were tossed in and some brave souls also dived in to save those who had hopefully avoided being crushed between the boat and the pier. Paul lost his grip as a wave of people marched onto the deck below him, making the boat bob unevenly. He fell on top of them with an exasperated scream.

Meanwhile, the fire drew even closer, licking the side of the log wall bordering the dock.

The whole island was ablaze—nothing but flames could be seen past the wall. Baz's heart pounded even harder when he noticed how few were the people clamouring at the dock, and an image of his friends and neighbours succumbing to the bushfire's relentless advance tortured his mind.

"Do we swim?" asked Elsa, tears flooding her eyes.

He teetered on the edge of the furthest pier with the only person who wanted to be there with him. He looked at Elsa and they kissed automatically like it was something they were supposed to do, or like they both knew that this was the end.

Then he shook his head, looking out at the bay and the expanse of orange-tinged water beyond, knowing they couldn't possibly swim to safety. Water, ironically the only thing that could stop the spreading fire, was now also playing a part in their imminent deaths.

Baz pulled Elsa close, thinking of Suzie and Alex at Mogood, thankful that at least they were safe. He kissed Elsa one last time, resigning himself to his fate.

But then he saw it—imperceptibly at first, but slowly becoming clearer in his vision. Something moved above the northern headland of Flat Rock Bay—a dark shadow against the black night. As the phenomenon drew closer and entered the raging fire's light, Baz's eyes went wide and he pointed fervently. "Look!" The yelling and screaming behind him continued, so he called again. "Everyone, look! Look!" A flash of lightning illuminated tall masts and sails.

Almost as one, the voice of the crowd died down as their salvation dawned on them. A flotilla of boats moved into the bay, approaching the dock under full sail. Foremost among them was the magnificent brig *Saviour*. The smaller vessels made for the piers, but they were still too far away—they weren't going to make it before the fire swallowed the docks. *Saviour* stopped some distance away—as close as her master dared bring her in the shallow waters.

130

The roaring bushfire lit them up clearly. A figure on *Saviour*'s deck waved wildly in Baz's direction. *Suzie!* She, along with the others on *Saviour*, were fervently motioning the Flat Rock Islanders to come to them.

"Go, go, go!" Baz said. "Strong swimmers, head to the tall ship and the other Mogood boats." His head whipped back so he could be heard by everyone behind him. "Only those who can't swim should use our boats. Now, move it!"

Seeing the wisdom of his words, most people complied with haste. Baz gave Elsa another kiss before telling her to go to Suzie.

"I love you," she said before squeezing his arms. But Baz didn't get to reply. She jumped into the water and started swimming out to the Mogood vessels.

Baz stayed back for as long as possible, making sure those who used the Flat Rock boats could get out safely. It seemed there were enough old sailors and hobbyists to get the passengers out.

"We okay," said a soft voice, and Baz turned to see Clem—covered in soot—smiling up at him from one of the boats.

"Clem, thank goodness—"

Clem gave a small wave and then had some men set the sails on his boat. Baz was alone on the pier. As he did one final visual sweep of the area, three Guardsmen rushed through the opened gateway of the burning dock wall. One was Matt Dean, carried by two comrades. His skin was red and blistering, and his clothes were singed and torn.

"Wait," Baz called out to Clem. As the flames licked at the dock, Baz helped the Guards lower the captain into the boat, and then Clem pulled away from the pier.

With the flames on his heels, Baz jumped into the water.

The coolness enveloped him—a welcome reprieve from the fire's hot proximity. Baz wasn't even aware of the swim, only the feeling of relief that he'd made it, along with all those he truly cared about. Before he knew it, *Saviour* was floating nearby. He grabbed one of the lines in the water and pulled himself up, his feet slipping on the low hull. When he made it to the deck he was met by the arms of his daughter, who held him close with tears in her eyes.

Amidst the blaze on the island and the massed group of hulls, masts, and sails all around him, he was just one man enveloped in the love of his daughter. Elsa stepped forward and Baz hugged her, too. Mayor Liam walked *Saviour*'s deck, checking on the rescued Islanders who lay soaked and panting. Deidre was among them— she gave Baz a weary thumbs-up to say she was okay.

"We saw the fire from Mogood," Suzie said, refusing to let go of her father. "There was a huge band of orange in the night sky. Mayor Liam organised every boat available to come and help. Alex is back at Mogood with the other local kids."

After a final sweep of the water, Mayor Liam gave the order to leave the bay. Captain Theo repeated the order, and his crew worked the rigging and shouted for the smaller vessels to follow.

"You came just in time," Baz told Suzie in a hoarse voice, and he suddenly felt weak. Adrenaline was catching up to him.

He sat on *Saviour*'s deck with Suzie and Elsa, looking back at the unstoppable force which had driven him from his home. He didn't know how many lives had perished in that all-consuming force of nature, and he didn't want to think about it. But one thing was certain: Flat Rock was no more. The island that had succeeded when every other had struggled—the island that had supported the economy of the entire South Coast . . . the same island whose mayor had sentenced Baz and Elsa to death—was no more.

But now Baz had his family, and that was all he ever wanted.

ABOUT THE AUTHOR

Nick Marone is a science fiction author based in Australia. *Fire Over Troubled Water* is his first published novella. You can learn more about his upcoming projects and a behind-the-scenes look at this story at nickmarone.com.

ABOUT DEADSET PRESS

Deadset Press is the publishing imprint for Aussie Speculative Fiction – a community aimed at supporting Australian and Kiwi authors. You can learn more at www.aussiespeculativefiction.com

ABOUT THE SERIES

Drowned Earth is a series of eight standalone novellas, set in a shared world.

Prequel: Shards of Silver by Alanah Andrews

Debbie is on board a ship when an asteroid collides with Antarctica, causing a tsunami. And it's heading her way…
(eBook Only: Free Download)

Submerged City by Austin P. Sheehan

Melbourne is under martial law, overseen by general Messinger—an extremist who believes the flood is God's retribution against the left-wing agenda…

The Rise by Sue-Ellen Pashley

The great Rise means that resources are scarce and not readily shared. But with her best friend's life at stake, along with some stranded refugees, Katie James knows she must prove there's more to being human than just existing. Even if that puts her on the same kill list.

Fire Over Troubled Water by Nick Marone

Despite winds, torrential rains, storms, and bushfires, a fresh water merchant searches for his lost daughter among the autonomous island communities of flooded eastern New South Wales.

Tides of War by Marcus Turner

After discovering a strange man in a row boat, Maria wages war on the lotus cities—clandestine floating communities off the coast of Victoria that are reserved for the wealthy.

The Jindabyne Secret by Jo Hart

With nothing but a map and a rickety solar truck, Jax journeys to the top secret fresh water facility at Lake Jindabyne—one of the few fresh water lakes left in Australia. What he discovers there could be the key to saving his whole community, as long as the government doesn't kill him first.

River of Diamonds by S. M. Isaac

Who would want to leave one of the last idyllic settlements since the Rise? Rosa has a map, a mercenary, and a hope to salvage a future for the world.

Salvaged by C.A. Clark

Cassie lives in the safe haven of academics on the anchored city of new Melbourne. After a diving incident she is rescued by a territorial beach combing gang who trade goods washed up by the frequent storms. Cassie wishes she had never taken her home for granted.

Emoto's Promise by Shel Calopa

Five hundred years after the flood, can Macie defeat the technology which has enslaved the last remaining humans in the walled city of Darwin?

ALSO BY DEADSET PRESS

Annual Anthologies

Beginnings: Australian Speculative Fiction Vol. 1

Journeys: Australian Speculative Fiction Vol. 2

Zodiac Series

Capricorn

Aquarius

Pisces

www.aussiespeculativefiction.com